GHOST SOLDIERS ON PARADE

Getting to his feet, Slocum thanked Kendricks for the grub and went to the mess hall door. The instant he opened the door, fog tried to sneak inside. He stepped outside into the night and heard a sound that sent a cold chill down his spine. His hand flashed to his Colt as he turned toward the parade grounds.

Through the gently drifting fog he caught sight of a man bent over as if the weight of the world bore down on his shoulders. Every step he took caused a new clank of heavy chains to sound.

"Hey!" Slocum dashed forward only to stop dead in his tracks when he saw a uniformed man—or he hoped it was a man. The unnaturally pale face turned dead eyes toward Slocum as an equally gray hand lifted to motion him away. Then the fog closed like a curtain, leaving Slocum to wonder what the hell he had just seen.

JAKE LOGAN

SLOCUM AND THE PRESIDIO PHANTOMS

J

JOVE BOOKS, NEW YORK

THE BERKLEY PUBLISHING GROUP
Published by the Penguin Group
Penguin Group (USA) Inc.
375 Hudson Street, New York, New York 10014, USA
Penguin Group (Canada), 10 Alcorn Avenue, Toronto, Ontario M4V 3B2, Canada
(a division of Pearson Penguin Canada Inc.)
Penguin Books Ltd., 80 Strand, London WC2R 0RL, England
Penguin Group Ireland, 25 St. Stephen's Green, Dublin 2, Ireland (a division of Penguin Books Ltd.)
Penguin Group (Australia), 250 Camberwell Road, Camberwell, Victoria 3124, Australia
(a division of Pearson Australia Group Pty. Ltd.)
Penguin Books India Pvt. Ltd., 11 Community Centre, Panchsheel Park, New Delhi—110 017, India
Penguin Group (NZ), Cnr. Airborne and Rosedale Roads, Albany, Auckland 1310, New Zealand
(a division of Pearson New Zealand Ltd.)
Penguin Books (South Africa) (Pty.) Ltd., 24 Sturdee Avenue, Rosebank, Johannesburg 2196,
South Africa

Penguin Books Ltd., Registered Offices: 80 Strand, London WC2R 0RL, England

This is a work of fiction. Names, characters, places, and incidents either are the product of the author's imagination or are used fictitiously, and any resemblance to actual persons, living or dead, business establishments, events, or locales is entirely coincidental.

SLOCUM AND THE PRESIDIO PHANTOMS

A Jove Book / published by arrangement with the author

PRINTING HISTORY
Jove edition / August 2005

Copyright © 2005 by The Berkley Publishing Group.

ISBN: 0-515-13986-6

JOVE®
Jove Books are published by The Berkley Publishing Group,
a division of Penguin Group (USA) Inc.,
375 Hudson Street, New York, New York 10014.
JOVE is a registered trademark of Penguin Group (USA) Inc.
The "J" design is a trademark belonging to Penguin Group (USA) Inc.

PRINTED IN THE UNITED STATES OF AMERICA

10 9 8 7 6 5 4 3 2 1

1

John Slocum liked San Francisco. The trouble was that San Francisco did not return the favor. He lengthened his stride until his boot heels clicked like Mexican castanets on the gaslit cobblestone street, then quickly ducked into an alley filled with rotting garbage. Slocum canted his head to one side and listened hard for the men hot on the trail after him. Not hearing any pursuit, he walked more slowly down the alley, picking his way through the darkness. The heavy fog had rolled in as soon as the sun had set, bringing a clammy cold that went well with the uneasy feeling someone was training a six-shooter at his spine.

More than once Slocum looked over his shoulder and saw nothing but the open mouth of the alley leading back to the street near Portsmouth Square. Then the fog drifted past and turned it into a billowy white mass that swirled and danced about as a horse-drawn carriage rattled past.

"Jumping at shadows," Slocum muttered to himself. He had tried to lose the men so intent on ventilating him most of the afternoon, but he was an intruder on their territory. If he had been in the Sierras he would have lost them within minutes. These city streets, with tumbledown buildings squatting alongside vast, wonderful gambling palaces, melodeons and deadfalls—these were the burrows the three gamblers called home.

Slocum took a step and stumbled, falling to one knee as he reached for the .36-caliber Colt Navy slung in his cross-draw holster. He had the six-gun half out before he saw there was no call for slinging lead around. He shoved the pistol back into the holster and tugged on the scrawny leg that had tripped him up. The leg pulled free. Slocum recoiled, then dropped the limb to dig around in the debris hiding the rest of the body. Wharf rats had feasted for some time, and now there was little left of the body.

"That's gonna be you, Slocum, if you don't pay up. You got the money or not? Me, it don't much matter. I'd as soon drill you as—"

Slocum located the voice coming from a dark, recessed doorway, feinted right and dived left. A slug ripped through the air, missing him by a country mile. He fetched up hard against the far wall of the alley, bounced and rolled back, fumbling to get his six-gun out so he could use it. More bullets kicked up dirt and debris around him.

"You wanna make it go down hard, Slocum? I don't care." Gabe Walensky's words carried a ring of truth. The gambler was a cold-blooded killer.

"I do. Stop shootin' at him, you damned fool. I want my money!"

The second voice chilled Slocum more than the first. Gabe's brother, Herk, had the look of a man who never lost a dime without someone being buried. He was as likely to torture Slocum to death as ask politely for what he thought was his due.

Slocum rolled into a ball, got his feet under him, then exploded upward to crash into the second gambler. Herk Walensky reeled back and fell heavily, landing atop the remains that had tripped up Slocum. The loud shouts and momentary confusion were all Slocum needed to beat a hasty retreat to the far end of the alley, leaving behind two furious gamblers.

He stumbled into a street completely veiled in fog and sought a gas streetlight to get his bearings. Slocum heard the soft scurry-scurry of huge black wharf rats all around, but right now he worried more about the human ones. Angry shouts echoed down the alley as the two distraught gamblers came after him. Slocum pressed his back against a clammy, cold wall and prayed for the fog to hide him. He was successful until a sudden gust of fetid wind from the harbor formed a perfectly clear patch around him, as if he stood in a spotlight on the Palace Theater stage.

"There! There's the son of a bitch!"

Slocum drew his six-shooter and waited for a clear shot. He wasn't going to be done in by this pair of tinhorn gamblers, especially since he didn't think he owed the money they sought so forcefully. A chip of wood from the wall beside his head flew off into the night. Slocum went into a gunfighter's crouch and bided his time. The first dark form that appeared from the cloaking fog got a bullet. Slocum knew instantly that he had only winged the gambler, but this was enough to put a tad of fear into the men. If it did nothing more than slow their pursuit, that would suit Slocum just fine. He backed away, hunting for another alley or even a crossing street. A quick glance at a battered sign told him he was going toward Portsmouth Square, where he had left his horse at a livery stable. If he reached Market Street he could get out of town and leave behind these no-account, back-shooting, bottom-dealing, lowlife snakes.

Slocum had got only a few yards when he realized the two gamblers had shouted for help and gotten it in spades. This was the city where the Sydney Ducks had reigned supreme in crime for years—until even more vicious gangs moved in and displaced them. Slocum listened to the muffled cries and shouted orders and reckoned he was up against a dozen or more owlhoots now. The odds were worse than sitting down at a green-felt table in a gambling emporium.

He walked as fast and quietly as he could, but the fog was drifting away, intent on betraying him. A loud cry went up behind, and he knew he would have to shoot it out with more men than he could possibly kill with the rounds remaining in his six-gun. He had not left his hotel thinking he would be caught up in a full-blown gunfight, but that was the way it had turned out.

"What's going on? Column, advance!"

Slocum jumped to the sidewalk as two dozen soldiers trotted by, their carbines coming up to firing position from where they had been carried in a slung position. During the war he had worn a butternut uniform and had not counted any man wearing Federal blue his friend, but now he was happy to see the patrol. He had no idea why they were in the middle of San Francisco, but he wasn't going to spit in Lady Luck's face. She had ignored him much of the day and into the evening. Now it was time for some good luck to come his way.

"You there, stand still!"

Slocum saw a sergeant and two troopers break from the column and circle him, pinning him against the cold stone wall of a bank.

"What're you up to?"

"Minding my own business. I heard some shots from that direction and thought I'd better hightail it the other way."

"Who's doing the shootin'?" demanded the sergeant. "I don't believe you ain't in this dustup all the way to your stubbly chin."

"They got clean away, Sergeant Thomassen," said an officer with a gleaming saber in his hand.

Slocum looked up at the man, and a slow smile came to his lips.

"You can throw your shoulder out of joint trying to use a

saber like that, Caleb. They're better suited for hacking beef carcasses."

"What?" The officer swung his skittish horse around and edged closer to Slocum, his blade swinging down menacingly. Then he pulled the blade back and let out a heartfelt laugh.

"As I live and breathe, is that you, John?"

"Reckon so, Caleb."

"Sergeant, stop pointing your rifle at this man. This is John Slocum. He's a friend of mine!"

"Yes, sir," Thomassen said with unconcealed irritation.

"How are you, John?"

"Feeling a mite better now that I don't have three carbines pointed at me." Slocum glanced back down the street, but the gamblers and their cronies had disappeared as if they had never existed. He knew they would return the instant the soldiers rode on, so he intended to invoke a privilege of friendship with Caleb Newcombe and get an escort to the stables to fetch his horse. It rankled to have to do this, but Slocum wasn't going to ride easy until he had a lot of miles between his back and San Francisco.

Slocum saw the officer look around uncomfortably, as if the men in his patrol were all spying on him.

"Get your men back to the post, Sergeant," Caleb Newcombe ordered. "I'll escort Mr. Slocum from this point."

"But, sir, we got to—"

"Do as you are ordered, Sergeant Thomassen," Newcombe said crisply.

"Yes, sir," the noncom said with ill grace. The sergeant formed his squad and got them walking away in good order, the clopping of horses' hooves disappearing quickly because of the curious sound-devouring property of the fog.

"I hadn't expected to come across *you* in the middle of San Francisco tonight," Caleb Newcombe said, dismounting. "You're looking good. You here for a reason or still just drifting to see what's behind the last sunset?"

"It's hard to find a place to settle down," Slocum allowed, "when there's so many sights waiting to be seen."

"You mean too many women to be ogled."

"Never was much on ogling," Slocum said, grinning. "Always was more on doing." He and Caleb had ridden together for a short while. "What about yourself? The last I saw of you was out in New Mexico. You were hunting for replacement scouts at Fort Bayard."

"Quelled the Apaches and got transferred here to the Presidio," Caleb said. "Got a promotion out of it, too."

"Captain's bars," Slocum said, nodding in approval. "Those are hard to come by after the war."

"There's not much need of military," Caleb agreed. "Especially after General Crook and the rest of his command did such a good job running down Geronimo and his Mescalero cutthroats." He looked around uneasily, again giving Slocum the impression the captain feared something moving just out of sight.

"You've got your duty, and I need to get my horse," Slocum said, nudging the officer along. "This is a good city, but it's time for me to go hunt for that new horizon you mentioned."

"John, could you ride with me a spell? I need advice from someone I trust. You were always the best scout I ever rode with."

"Saved your hide more 'n once, too," Slocum said, reminding the captain of his obligations.

"What's one more favor when you're right, you've have saved my life. This time you can help salvage my sanity. John, I think I'm going crazy." The captain looked around again, his fingers drumming nervously on the handle of his saber. Slocum had ridden with Newcombe for several months and had never seen him so edgy, even in the face of a spirited Indian attack when they had trailed a small band of Apaches into Dog Canyon north of Oro Grande, the site of more than one massacre. This agitation made Slocum come to a decision he knew was dead wrong, but curiosity drove him to find what was eating away at Caleb Newcombe so.

"Sounds serious. Let me get my horse so we can talk it over." Slocum felt a tad of uneasiness remaining on the San Francisco streets with the fog giving cover to anyone who might take a potshot at him. The gamblers had been mighty het up over the supposed debt he owed them. Getting their revenge for both the debt and the brief shoot-out might go a ways toward evening the score in their minds—and Slocum wanted to avoid that.

The two walked through the preternaturally quiet streets until Slocum reached the stables, saddled his horse and mounted, riding alongside his old friend. As they rode along, Slocum cast a sidelong look at Caleb. Time had not been kind to him. Although they were about the same age, Newcombe looked ten years older. A hint of gray shot through his hair and wrinkles that had not come from too much merriment wrinkled his forehead and the area around his eyes. Caleb Newcombe was a man who worried far more than was good for him.

"Tell me about it," Slocum said, letting the captain lead the way. He wasn't sure where they rode, but it seemed to be away from the Barbary Coast, where he had run afoul of the tinhorn gamblers. The San Francisco waterfront was no fit place for man or beast, but that was where Slocum had spent most of his time since arriving in the city with his partner.

His now-dead partner.

". . . adjutant for the past two months," Caleb was saying. Slocum had been remembering more than listening.

"You said your pa's the post commander?"

"Father got promoted to colonel more 'n five years ago. He had expected to receive a brigadier's appointment by now, but as I said, there's not much need for senior officers anymore."

Something in the way Caleb spoke of his pa warned Slocum of less than cordial relations.

"He ask for you to be his adjutant?"

"No," Newcombe said stiffly, "but relations with my father isn't my problem."

"Something's got you mighty spooked," Slocum said. His eyes widened when he saw Caleb's reaction. The man's hand went to his holstered pistol, but he checked himself before he drew. Even controlling himself, the officer did not relax. "What's wrong, Caleb? You're jumping at shadows. You were always easygoing before." For Slocum's taste, Caleb Newcombe had been a little too easygoing, taking his time and letting opportunities escape him.

"I . . . I think it's best if you determine the problem for yourself so I don't prejudice you."

"If you're not willing to spit it out, how'm I supposed to find out?"

"Talk to the enlisted men. Don't bother with the officers on the post. They all think I'm already crazy, but the men—they're the ones who most concern me."

"You always looked after your men," Slocum said. "I remember that foray into the Guadalupe Mountains. You spent most of the patrol half starved, but your men always got first dibs on any rations."

"They fought well. They deserved whatever I could do for them."

"You should have gotten a medal for that skirmish at Rattlesnake Springs," Slocum said. "But you sent in the recommendations for your two noncoms."

"Getting the job done is more important than medals."

"Is that the way your pa sees it, too?"

"He isn't the problem, John," Caleb said. "There. There's the entrance to the Presidio. It's the best-run post I've ever served at, but then there's not much action beyond Sunday parades. What activity there is gets funneled past Fort Point instead."

"The fort down on the shore?"

"It was built before the war to protect the harbor. I don't have much to do with that section of the Presidio command."

Slocum wondered at Newcombe's actual duties. If he were adjutant of the post, he had to see everything that his commanding officer—his father—did. Slocum wondered if this might be part of Caleb's problems, although he appeared less concerned with what went on at Fort Point than with his men's morale higher on the hill in the Presidio itself, overlooking the Pacific Ocean as well as San Francisco Bay.

They trotted to the gate, where two sentries came out, rifles at the ready. It surprised Slocum that two guards had been posted. It was even more startling to see another pair just inside the gate, also with readied rifles. This kind of alertness was appropriate to a post expecting to be attacked by a powerful enemy force.

"Report!" barked Newcombe.

"Sir, Sergeant Thomassen and his patrol returned to post twenty minutes ago. They reported nothing unusual."

"What about here, on the post?"

This question caused Slocum to swivel in the saddle to study his friend more carefully. Newcombe was drawn and jumpy. The query carried a desperation that Slocum had never expected to hear from a man with combat experience and now performing garrison duty. Caleb Newcombe was scared to death.

"Nothing, sir. We don't reckon the fog's gonna lift anytime soon, though."

"Very good." The officer started to ride onto the post, then drew rein. "This gentleman is John Slocum. You will give him full respect and answer any questions he might ask. Is that clear?"

"That order go for all the company, sir?"

"It does."

"Understood, sir." The sentry—a corporal—nodded warily in Slocum's direction. His eyes took in the newcomer, as if he was uncertain how to respond or what to make of someone being given military courtesy when he was obviously a civilian. Slocum wondered what the U.S. Army corporal would think about giving such courtesy to a man who had ridden with Quantrill's Raiders as a captain.

"Why so many guards on the gate?" Slocum asked as he and Caleb rode down a road with neatly trimmed hedges on either side, directly to the post HQ. From what he saw the entire Presidio was in tiptop condition, showing that, in spite of garrison duty's being dull as dishwater, the elder Newcombe kept a tight rein on his men.

"That has to do with why you're helping me, John. I'll tell you everything, but after you've asked some questions of the men. I'll issue orders so you can go wherever you want on the post. And I can billet you in the visiting officers' quarters. The IG is supposed to make a visit in a week or so but until then, no one is staying there."

Slocum said nothing. He had not expected this to take long, but the offer of free room and board appealed to him, even though the chow was likely to be army mess hall quality. Considering what he had lived on in the past, even this would seem like a banquet fit for a king.

"Thinking on it, I can't remember when I ate last. Could I chow down, then get to asking what's got folks riled?"

"Go on. Over there's the mess hall. I have reports to finish and will be in my office. First floor, down the corridor to the left." Caleb made a vague gesture indicating where he would be toiling far into the night.

"Figure by now everyone knows I can ask all the questions I want?"

"What? Oh, yes, probably so. The only thing that travels faster than a bullet on an army post is gossip." For the first time Caleb smiled. A little, not much, but it showed that some of the man Slocum had known in New Mexico remained.

Slocum dismounted and tethered his horse in front of the post headquarters, then sauntered to the mess hall. Odors of baking bread reached him, making his mouth water. He climbed the three steps and pushed into the hall. He and Caleb had been right about the captain's order reaching every ear on the post. One of the gate guards spoke quietly to a cook, who turned and looked in Slocum's direction.

"Figgered you'd come on over to get some of my chow, Mr. Slocum. Set yerse'f down and I'll rustle up some grub. I'm 'bout finished bakin' bread for morning mess. And some of my special coffee. You need a cup or two of it in you if you want to stay alert."

"Worked on a chuck wagon?" asked Slocum.

"Poisoned so many cowboys Kendricks had to join the army. Ain't nobody else'd take him," joked the private who had brought the news about a stranger riding onto the post with their adjutant.

Slocum settled at the end of the table and got a plate of stew and some of the freshly baked bread dropped in front of him. His mouth watered at the sight of such good chow. He looked up and saw the private heading for the door.

"Come on back, Private," Slocum called. "You heard Captain Newcombe's orders. I might as well get some work done while I'm being poisoned." He grinned at the cook, who snorted and turned back to his work. But Slocum saw the cook was pleased at the appraisal of his culinary output. That meant it was probably as good as it smelled. Slocum forked in a large hunk of beef and knew right away that Kendricks had never killed anyone, not with cooking this outstanding, unless his victims had eaten themselves into an early grave.

"I got to return to my post. The colonel'd have my hide if he finds I'm not watchin' the gate."

"In spite of what Captain Newcombe ordered?" Slocum saw the conflict on the man's young face, and knew this wasn't the first time that Caleb's orders had conflicted with those of his father—or maybe it was the other way around. There might be a struggle over who actually commanded the soldiers at the Presidio.

"Sorry, sir. I cain't rightly decide this fer myself."

"I won't keep you long. Sit. And, Kendricks, get some more coffee for me." Slocum pushed his tin cup toward the private, who hesitantly took it. Kendricks grumbled and went to fetch another, to replace the coffee laced with whiskey that Slocum had given away to the private.

"Why so many soldiers on the gate? I saw a roving patrol around the post perimeter, too."

"You did? Gosh, they's our best men. Ain't nobody'd spotted them 'fore now. You must be a powerful good scout. Leastwise, that's what's bein' said 'bout you."

Slocum had guessed that there were such patrols, especially after encountering Sergeant Thomassen's in the city. The military did not enforce law in the city, not when the San Francisco police were legally entrusted with that chore.

"What's going on here?" Slocum continued to eat, watching Kendricks from the corner of his eye since the cook was eavesdropping. His reaction would count as much as the private's answer.

"Not much, sir. I mean, we ain't seen much. Not all of us."

"But some have seen it, haven't they?"

" 'It'?" Kendricks laughed. "You mean 'them'!" The cook came over and stood behind the private.

"More than one? Tell me about it," Slocum said.

"Ghosts. Danged phantoms, thass what," the private said. He gulped down the hot spiked coffee and choked on it. "I ain't seen any, but Kendricks has."

"So?" Slocum mopped up the gravy with his bread as he watched both soldiers carefully for any sign they might be lying. The private showed both a little concern and a lot of fright. Kendricks was made of sterner stuff, being older and more experienced. But his face blanched when he said, "I saw 'em, Mr. Slocum. A whole damn army of phantoms. Haints! They walked across the parade ground as plain as day."

"During the day?"

"No, at night," the private said. "They don't come 'less it's all foggy and dark. That's why we got so many guards posted tonight. This is about perfect for 'em to show up."

"That's true," Kendricks confirmed. "I seen them, maybe twenty of them, not a week back in weather just like this. All quiet,'cept for the clanking chains."

"Chains?"

"Chains clanking at their ankles, and they was groaning like they was hell-bound souls."

"Tell him 'bout the demons, Kendricks. Go on, tell him."

"And demons. There were these four demons poking and prodding those lost souls."

"What did the demons look like?" Slocum asked. He finished his plate of stew and wondered if he ought to interrupt the story—the tall tale—for another serving. The remainder of his coffee would have to do him, since Kendricks was launching into a detailed description of the demons herding the lost souls. From the private's expression, Slocum figured Kendricks was embroidering the description with every telling.

"They was dead soldiers. Wore uniforms. Union uniforms of men killed here at the Presidio. Might be they were takin' Reb prisoners to the pits of hell."

"Never a shot fired against a Confederate force here," Slocum said. "Where'd the Reb soldiers die?"

"I wasn't 'bout to go and ask!" Kendricks sounded sincerely shocked that Slocum considered this at all. Slocum thought hard as he drained his coffee. Kendricks might be quite a storyteller around a cattle drive campfire, but his re-counting, no matter how exaggerated, carried his convic-tion with it. He believed he had seen ghosts.

The private believed Kendricks. Slocum reckoned most others at the Presidio believed because Kendricks did.

"Anyone else see them?"

Kendricks and the private exchanged looks. The private swallowed hard and then said, "Mr. Slocum, I'm 'bout the only one who *ain't* seen the ghosts. All three of my buddies at the front gate, they all's seen the ghosts."

"At the same time you did, Kendricks?"

"A half dozen times, over the past three months. Them phantoms started their parade in early March. 'Bout the time the fog gets worst."

"Is there a cemetery around here?" Slocum asked.

"Surely is," the private said. "We thought of that right away and posted men all 'round it, but that don't prevent the phantoms from goin' on parade."

"Get on back to your post," Slocum said. "And you, Kendricks, you can get me another slice of that bread. With butter, if you have it."

"Fresh-churned yesterday mornin'. I got me a whole passel of men workin' off punishment duty."

Slocum drank another cup of coffee as he ate his but-tered bread, thinking hard. Such gossip destroyed the morale of a post in short order. That it had been three months and the men hadn't started deserting was a tribute to either the colonel's or Caleb's command, but such ru-mors had to be scotched or they would eventually wear down even the best commander.

Or *had* men deserted?

Getting to his feet, Slocum thanked Kendricks for the grub and went to the mess hall door. The instant he opened the door, fog tried to sneak inside. He stepped outside into the night and heard a sound that sent a cold chill down his spine. His hand flashed to his Colt as he turned toward the parade grounds.

Through the gently drifting fog he caught sight of a man bent over as if the weight of the world bore down on his shoulders. Every step he took caused a new clank of heavy chains to sound.

"Hey!" Slocum dashed toward the man, only to stop dead in his tracks when he saw a second, uniformed man— or he hoped it was a man. The unnaturally pale face of this second man turned dead eyes toward Slocum as an equally gray hand lifted to motion him away. Then the fog closed like a curtain, leaving Slocum to wonder what the hell he had just seen.

2

Slocum drew his six-shooter and turned around, listening hard, hunting for something to shoot. The fog muffled sound, but he heard something moving in the direction he thought the ghosts—or whatever they had been—went. He took a step that way, then froze as a bloodcurdling cry cut through the silence.

Like a compass needle, Slocum moved in on the sound. Whoever had screamed wasn't likely to be one of the garrison, not unless the army had started recruiting women. A second cry, more muffled but still shrill, guided him forward to almost crash into a woman.

His arms circled her and she spun about, then began fighting, clawing and struggling to get free.

"Whoa, settle down," he cautioned. "What's wrong?"

"I . . . I . . . Who are you?" She pushed hard against him, sending Slocum back a step. Her brown eyes took in the drawn six-gun and the fact that he was not dressed in a blue uniform. "You're not a soldier. Why'd you scare me like that?"

"I was in the mess hall," Slocum said. "I came out and you screamed. What happened?" He neglected to mention seeing what might have been the phantoms that were scar-

16

ing the men in the garrison. Slocum needed to think about what he had actually seen, since he didn't believe in ghosts. But there had been something—someone—moving through the fog.

"What were you doing there?" she asked. "Pilfering? Who are you?"

Slocum finally had the opportunity to study the woman more closely. Her brown eyes flashed angrily, but this heightened her already great beauty. A pile of hair on her head had been dislodged and canted to one side, giving her a wild look. Her tanned face proved she was not the one Slocum had seen, even if she had somehow shed the Union jacket he had seen the apparition wearing. He cast his eyes from head to toe and back and liked what he saw. She was shapely and dressed modestly, although her clothing was somewhat disordered. When she realized how closely he studied her, she sniffed loudly and tried patting her hair back into shape. It only caused a new cascade of chestnut hair to fall across her eyes.

"My name's Slocum. Who might you be?"

"The one you are menacing with that six-shooter, that's who," she said hotly. Her fright was vanishing, replaced with anger. Slocum wondered if the anger was directed at him or if he was simply a convenient target for her to hide her reaction to . . . what?

"What'd you see that frightened you so?" he asked.

"Nothing. I frightened myself. I thought I had gotten lost in the fog."

"Not bad," Slocum said, holstering his six-gun. "Not bad for a lie right off the top of your head."

"How dare you insult me!"

"What really happened?" His voice carried a steel edge to it now that forced the woman to consider him more closely.

Before she answered, Caleb Newcombe rushed to their side.

"Thank God I found you in the accursed fog. Are you all right, Glory?"

"Glory had quite a scare because of what she saw," Slocum said. He was rewarded with an upturned chin and a flounce as the brunette tried to leave in a huff. Slocum grabbed her arm and spun her back around. "What did you see, Glory?"

"Slocum," came Caleb's warning. The captain stepped between them, forcing Slocum to release the woman's arm. "Allow me to introduce my sister, Miss Glory Newcombe."

"Pleased to meet you," Slocum said with only a hint of sarcasm in his voice. "Now what the hell made you scream like that?"

"John!"

"You wanted me to find out what's wrong around here, Caleb. Your sister might shed some light on what's otherwise a mighty murky picture."

"I didn't see anything, Caleb," the woman said. Slocum saw she was lying, but her brother accepted the words at face value. "I got turned around and then *he* came out of the fog waving his six-gun around like a madman. Of course I was distraught."

"She screamed before I found her," Slocum said, knowing it would do nothing to convince Caleb Newcombe.

"Maybe it was about the same time," Glory said. "I don't want to cause you any trouble, Mr. Slocum."

"It's a little chilly out here," Caleb said. "Let's go to my office and finish this discussion."

Slocum looked over his shoulder, trying to get his bearings. He had seen two men in the fog and wanted to pursue, but if the sentries didn't catch them, he might not have any better luck. Still he would never know unless he tried.

"My office. Now, John, now." Caleb Newcombe's tone showed he wasn't going to argue the point. Reluctantly, Slocum followed Glory and her brother into the three-story brick HQ building. The instant he stepped inside he felt his shirt plaster itself to his body. He hadn't realized how damp he had been outside until the added heat from the building caused the moisture to condense against his skin.

He couldn't help noticing that the same thing had happened to Glory Newcombe, though with more delightful results. She felt his eyes on her and glanced over her shoulder. Her brown eyes widened slightly when she saw the play of muscles in his strong arms and across his broad chest, even as he saw how her white linen blouse conformed perfectly to her conical breasts, capped with the hard, large buttons of her nipples.

"In here," Caleb said, holding a door open to a corner office. Slocum waited for Glory to find a chair before he sat across the desk from Caleb. In this position, Slocum got a good look at both brother and sister. He saw the family similarities now that the light was better. Both had high cheekbones, and the general shape of their faces was identical. Caleb's russet-colored hair had developed that streak of gray and dark circles under his eyes robbed him of any handsomeness to match his sister's beauty. If Slocum had to guess, Caleb was at least ten years older. Try as he might, he couldn't remember Caleb mentioning any relatives, other than his father, when they had fought the Apaches together in New Mexico Territory.

He wondered why Caleb had never mentioned Glory.

Caleb Newcombe heaved a deep sigh, then slammed his fist down hard on the desk, startling Glory and annoying Slocum.

"What the hell do you think you were doing, John? This is my sister you were scaring the dickens out of."

"Caleb, watch your language," Glory scolded in a tone better suited to a mother disciplining a young child.

"This is serious business, Glory. I don't care if you don't agree. The men are—"

"The men," she taunted, "are fools. Superstitious fools. Who knows which of them concocted this wild story of ghosts marching around on the parade grounds, but it's got all of them seeing phantoms."

"I saw them, too," Slocum said.

Caleb stared at him, mouth agape. Glory's lips thinned, and she turned away, crossing her arms and closing off to him entirely.

"You did?" Caleb's voice came out choked and distant.

"I saw something on the parade grounds," Slocum said. "I'm not saying they were ghosts, but something was out there. Before I could go after them, Glory screamed and I went to see if I could be of help."

"Oh, right," Glory said sarcastically, "as if I needed any help. I explained to you what happened. I got turned around in the fog, then you came out waving that big gun of yours around. *That's* what startled me into crying out."

Slocum said nothing more, knowing that arguing wouldn't solve anything. He saw how Glory eyed him, her brown eyes boring into his green ones. He refused to break contact, and she eventually turned to her brother.

"This is absurd, Caleb. You know what Father thinks of your silly obsession with phantoms and all that spiritualistic claptrap."

"The men think there're ghosts. It doesn't matter if there really are. It upsets them and disrupts good discipline."

"So you asked him to investigate? What is he? One of those Pinkerton detectives?"

Slocum found himself wondering more and more about Glory Newcombe. Her tone carried a combination of contempt and something else. Fear? He thought so.

"What are you so afraid of, Miss Newcombe?" Slocum asked. He might have poked her with a pin from the way she jumped.

"I'm afraid of my brother making a complete fool of himself. It's hard enough to gain promotion in today's army. This will be a black mark on his record that will never be overlooked."

"By the inspector general?"

Again Glory Newcombe jumped.

"You know he's coming next week? My," Glory said, turning to her brother again, "you tell him everything, don't you?"

"This isn't any of your concern, Glory. It's a military matter. I trust John completely." Caleb heaved a sigh. "He saved my life more than once."

"Oh, one of those New Mexico ruffians." Her appraising gaze changed a mite, or so Slocum thought. He wondered at what went on in that pretty head of hers.

"I want to get out and find where they went."

"You can't track them in the fog, John," protested Caleb. "It's too dangerous. Besides, if they were on the parade grounds, there will be too many tracks for you to find the right trail. We had a lengthy assembly this afternoon, before the fog came in."

"Preparing for the IG's visit," Glory cut in.

"I still want to try," Slocum said. He didn't cotton much to wandering around in the dense fog, but saw his chance of getting answers and putting Caleb's fears to rest diminishing with every passing minute. Slocum had seen men in the fog. What they were doing was the real question he wanted to answer.

"I'd go with you, but I have to stay here for another hour. The colonel wanted a meeting before morning mess with his staff to go over, uh, matters." Caleb looked uneasy and, as much as Slocum wondered why the post commander had scheduled a meeting at this early hour, he said nothing. Caleb made brushing motions with his hand as he said, "Go on. I need to finish a report before the meeting. Don't get into too much trouble, John."

"I'm certain he is accustomed to doing that very thing,"

Glory said, but this time her voice was lilting, almost teasing. She gave him a coy look that would have melted the sternest of hearts. Slocum was not in the least surprised when she said, "Would you be so kind as to escort me to my quarters, Mr. Slocum?"

The invitation was obvious, but not to her brother. Caleb had already turned back to his paperwork, muttering to himself as he went down long columns of numbers.

"I'm sure your brother can find an armed detachment of soldiers who can do that, Miss Newcombe." Before she could react, Slocum was out of the office and halfway through the outer door. He wondered if Glory might be fuming mad at his refusal, but her sudden changes of heart since he had stumbled on her in the fog were confusing.

Slipping into the dank night, Slocum got his bearings and returned to the mess hall, then turned in the direction where he had spotted the chained figure and the ghostly, ghastly white guard with it. Striding purposefully, he paced off the number of steps he had taken in his futile pursuit before, then knelt and studied the ground. Tracking might not be as difficult as Caleb had made it out to be. The moisture in the air had caused the ground to turn soft. Slocum had left obvious footprints from the mess hall both times.

But his search turned up no sign of new footprints other than his own. He came across a set of depressions that might have been recent, but he could not tell for certain. Definitely made by a soldier's boot, but there was only one and it might have been left behind by some sentry pacing his guard route. Of the chained man he had seen, there was no trace, not even crushed grass. It was as if the prisoner had drifted just above the ground, not touching down hard enough to leave a mark on mother earth.

Sense of smell thwarted and the roiling fog robbing him of other important senses, Slocum blundered along almost blind, trying to follow a virtually nonexistent trail. He kept moving in the direction taken by the . . . things he had seen, gradually beginning to doubt his eyes.

What if they *had* been ghosts?

He saw the Presidio cemetery off to his left as he made his way along a well-trodden path that led downhill toward San Francisco. Without any clues to go on, Slocum kept moving in the faint hope of finding the pale-faced soldier or the manacled prisoner. His stride lengthened when he heard voices in the distance, almost drowned out by the lapping of waves. Not sure where he was, Slocum plunged ahead and found himself on a broad cobblestoned plain not far from the shore of the bay.

Slocum had taken several paces toward the voices when he saw a four-story-high gray wall looming before him. He stopped and tried to make out details. Narrow windows on the first floor revealed nothing, but the crenellations along the top showed the ugly snouts of heavy cannon.

Fort Point.

"Halt! Stop or we'll shoot!"

Slocum swung around, his hand starting for his six-gun. But he checked the move when he saw two soldiers with Spencers leveled at him, ready to fire. He could never have cleared leather and gotten off two shots before they killed him, even if he had wanted to shoot it out with a pair of sentries.

"Whoa, hold your horses," Slocum called. "I don't mean you any harm."

"Git those hands of yers up in the air, away from that dogleg on yer hip." One guard moved to the right, circling to catch Slocum in a crossfire if he tried to throw down on them. But Slocum wasn't going up against two soldiers who were obviously veterans and well-trained in their duties.

"Pluck his six-shooter from his holster, Ned," the older of the pair said. "We'll get him to the lieutenant and see what he thinks."

"I was looking for . . . a ghost," Slocum said. He saw

how the two men stiffened. "What do you know about them? Captain Newcombe's sent me to track them down."

"Captain Newcombe?" The two men smirked at the name. "Not the colonel?"

"The adjutant," Slocum said, wondering at their reaction.

"Might be true," one allowed. "The captain's likely to have hired some drifter to chase them haints."

Slocum started to say that he had seen two with his own eyes and they were not ghosts, but he decided to veer in a different direction.

"Either of you seen the ghosts?"

"Naw, neither of us," the older said, relaxing a bit, though his rifle still pointed in Slocum's direction and the other man had taken his Colt Navy from its holster. "Them boys up on the hill, the ones in the Presidio, they take a nip too much at times, we think. Ain't that so, Ned?"

"Reckon so," said the other soldier, who had jammed Slocum's pistol into his broad leather belt. "They spin the wildest stories. Long lines of haints all hunched over, chained together and moanin' for their eternal souls. And sometimes they see wimmen 'stead of men. It's almost worth gettin' them sots all likkered up to hear their tall tales."

"But you've never seen these ghosts?"

Both men laughed.

"We don't drink on duty, mister. And you can tell Captain Newcombe that."

"What kind of stories do the soldiers at the Presidio spin?"

"That big, burly sergeant. What's his name, Ned?"

"You mean Thomassen?"

"He's the one," Ned said, intent on his recitation. "I swear, he's got more stories of ghosts than any two of the rest. He's the gent to ask if you want to hear cock-and-bull stories to make the hair on the back of yer neck go all tingly."

"Quite the spinner of tales, that one. Now git movin'. We got to turn you over to the officer of the watch."

Slocum let them prod him in the direction of the huge pile of stone. Ned banged on a small wood door that eventually creaked open on unoiled hinges to admit them to a narrow corridor. Slocum's shoulders brushed the walls on either side until they reached the central courtyard. Above, running all around on the second and third stories, were walkways for the artillerists and their heavy cannon.

"That way," Ned said, directing Slocum toward an office partway down the southern wall of the fort. There an officer sat, rocking back in his chair, highly polished boots hiked up on his desk. He glanced over when the two guards herded Slocum inside.

"What'd you fish out of the bay this time?" The officer dropped his newspaper and got his feet under him.

"A prowler just outside, Lieutenant. Not sure what the varmint was up to."

"Said he works for Captain Newcombe, up on the hill."

"Do you, now?" The officer worked to hold back a smirk, unconsciously mimicking the reaction of his two guards upon hearing Slocum's story. "You won't mind if I send a courier to the Presidio and ask, will you? Otherwise, you might rot here at Fort Point until we get around to charging you with criminal trespass."

"The sooner the better," Slocum said, not wanting to spend even a minute of his life in a cramped prison cell. He knew from hard experience what military stockades were like and had no reason to suppose Fort Point's was any different.

It took Caleb Newcombe more than an hour before he came to alibi Slocum out of the six-by-eight-foot cell.

3

"Thanks for getting me out of the jailhouse," Slocum said as he trudged up the hill toward the Presidio beside Caleb Newcombe.

"I ought to have warned you," Caleb said. "Wait, I did warn you, and you ignored me. It would have served you right if I'd left you to rot in that miserable stockade." For several paces the captain said nothing, then, "What'd you learn, John? You went after the apparitions you saw. What did you find?"

"Not much, but unless I miss my guess, you're concerned about desertion because of soldiers seeing the ghosts. Is that why you wanted me to look into whatever it is wandering around at night in the fog?"

"Yes," Caleb said, obviously distraught. "The inspector general will go over our records when he arrives and, frankly, we have an almost twenty percent desertion rate. That ranks us near the top in the entire army, if not the utter worst. My father will never be able to survive such a report."

"What about yourself? You're the adjutant, and it would reflect real bad on you, too."

"My career would be over, but then I may well have

reached the highest rank I'll ever see anyway. The army's different, John, very different these days." Caleb frowned and looked at the ground as he slogged along the path leading back to the Presidio HQ. His shoulders were slumped, and he walked more like an old man than an officer in his prime.

"You're worried more about your pa not getting his star." Slocum heard the resignation in Caleb's voice when it came to his own career. The only reason he would be so upset about morale and the desertions, if he thought his days in the army were numbered, was for someone else.

"It wasn't fair. Not at all. He was passed over for no reason relating to his abilities. There are strong political currents flowing against him, and they all come from the Western Region HQ. You know how General Sheridan can be. Look what he did to Ben Grierson."

Slocum was glad for more than one reason not to be in the U.S. Army. The favoritism that ruled in the military west of the Mississippi after the war was bad enough, but when decent, even brilliant officers like Colonel Grierson down at Fort Davis were constantly passed over because of a feud between Phil Sheridan and William Sherman, efficiency and morale had to suffer.

"What do you think is spooking your men?" Slocum asked.

"I've tried to find out, John. I have! Nothing works. I don't—didn't—believe in ghosts, but now I'm doubting my own senses. I post men to watch, especially during foggy nights like this, and they either see nothing . . . or they see the phantoms. Most likely they don't show up for muster the next morning, if they spot the ghosts."

"Desertion?"

"What else?"

Slocum frowned in thinking on this as they went back into Caleb's office.

"Are you certain they desert, or might there be some foul play going on?"

Caleb snorted in disgust and shook his head. "They all go AWOL; their bunk mates testify to that. If there had been anything such as you're suggesting, it would have been obvious. No, they see something and then they high-tail it away from the Presidio and their careers. I've got warrants out on nine men already, just in Sergeant Thomassen's platoon."

"You haven't found any of them?"

"Not a trace. Not a one's been seen after they leave."

"Do they take their gear?"

"So far, they have," Caleb said dispiritedly. "No telling where they are now, or if they'll ever be caught."

"Chances are against it," Slocum said. "Anything else happening on the post that's out of the ordinary?"

"Some theft from the mess, but that's not so unusual. Every post where I've ever been stationed has had petty pilferage. If anything, ours is less than other commands, probably because Kendricks keeps such a close watch on supplies. I'm certain this will be the one bright spot when the IG comes, if he bothers to get as far as taking inventory of our supplies."

"Have you seen the ghosts more than once in an evening?" asked Slocum after a bit of thought. "Were the ones spotted tonight early or late?"

"I suppose early, but yes, there have been several nights when my men have seen the phantoms twice. Never more than that."

"Tonight will be a second showing," Slocum said, heaving to his feet. "Grab a rifle. We're going to catch ourselves a ghost."

"A rifle? That doesn't do any good. Some of my men have tried shooting them and—"

"And what?" demanded Slocum.

"The bullets go right through the ghosts." Caleb was a tad paler than he had been.

"You're not scared of them, are you?"

"No," the officer said, finding some backbone at last. He went to a rack, pulled down a rifle and looked at Slocum.

"You keep that one. I'll stick with my six-gun." Slocum rested his hand on the ebony handle. He trusted the Colt more than he did army-issue carbines. He waited for Caleb to settle his nerves, then stopped his friend when Caleb started to leave by the front door.

"Out back," Slocum said. "We'll circle and see what we can rustle up."

"Don't use words like that," Caleb said, a small smile finally dancing on his lips. "There hasn't been a cattle rustling in San Francisco in more years than I can remember. It'd be hell if the IG got here just as one got recorded."

"Don't reckon to rustle *cattle*," Slocum said, although in his day he had done his share. "Figure on finding something with fewer legs and more firepower."

They exited the HQ and worked to the west, heading down the forested slope leading to the Pacific Ocean a hundred yards away before Slocum motioned for Caleb to halt. He put his finger to his lips to keep the officer silent, then settled down on his haunches, half hidden behind low bushes. Caleb joined him. For over an hour they crouched, seeing only an occasional patrol the captain had set to roving through the Presidio. The soldiers never spotted them, and Caleb grumbled under his breath about carelessness, but Slocum knew it would take more than a casual patrol— and one performed by frightened men—to flush them.

When the fog began rolling in more heavily, Caleb whispered, "It's almost daybreak. How much longer?"

"Tide's in, isn't it?"

"Ought to be."

"Not long," Slocum said, shifting his aching legs to get

circulation back in them. As he moved, he heard distant clanking. Caleb grabbed his arm, but Slocum motioned him to silence. He moved a few feet to one side to get a better view of the steep slope leading down to the Pacific Ocean from the hilltop Presidio. Slocum wasn't sure if it was his imagination making out a faint trail through the wooded area or if it really existed. But he was positive when he saw movement between two trees, smack dab in the middle of what he took to be the trail.

He reached out and held back Caleb. The captain had lifted his rifle, preparing to fire.

"Wait," Slocum whispered. "I want a better look." His heart leapt into his throat when he saw the bent figures trudging along, chained at the ankles. Five men barely visible in the fog and darkness shuffled along, with two white-faced, black-eyed ghosts carrying rifles moving on either side of the single-file line.

Caleb broke free and yelled, "Halt!"

The ghostly figures raised their rifles and pointed them in his direction. He fired at a distance of ten yards. Slocum knew the officer was a crack shot from their days in New Mexico. At this range Caleb could not miss.

He missed.

Slocum whipped out his Colt Navy and fired, only to be driven to the ground by the two ghosts firing at him with their very unghostlike weapons. Leaves flew all around as Slocum flattened himself on the ground.

"Those aren't any phantoms," gasped out Caleb, scrambling to get into position to fire again. He pushed aside a shrub and rested his rifle barrel on a limb. He fired and missed again. "Damn!" he cried in frustration. "I don't know what's wrong. The lead ghost was dead in my sights!"

Caleb Newcombe suddenly grunted and bent forward, clutching his belly.

"Caleb!" Slocum rolled to his friend's side and saw a

dark splotch on the officer's uniform, seeping between his fingers as he tried futilely to stanch the blood.

"Get 'em, John. Go get 'em!"

Slocum thought the captain would be all right for a few minutes—long enough to bring down the two men with rifles. He didn't believe in ghosts, no matter what his eyes told him. Real ghosts had no need for real rifles shooting real bullets. Slocum scooped up Caleb's fallen rifle and lit out after the "ghosts," working more by sound than sight because the fog had thickened and now swirled about, plunging the Presidio into a gray otherness that was more than a little disconcerting.

Slocum tried to follow the footprints, but they were indistinct and he had to guess at the path. Striding faster, he went toward the cemetery and almost stumbled over a gravestone in the fog. He slowed, turned slowly and tried to get his bearings. In the distance he heard small, pitiful, trapped-animal sounds. He made his way through the tombstones in that direction. A vagrant breeze parted the fog enough for him to see one of the blue-clad ghosts. The line of prisoners he guarded faded away as they shuffled onward into the fog, but Slocum had one decent shot. The rifle came easily to his shoulder, fit snugly, was aimed well—and he fired.

The recoil was less than he expected. And he missed, just as Caleb Newcombe had.

The ghost turned and made a mocking gesture before vanishing. Slocum lowered his rifle and stared at it in wonder. He had been a sniper during the war, one of the best who'd ever fought for the CSA. Sitting on a hill all day, waiting for the momentary flash of Federal brass or braid, the careful squeezing of the trigger, the recoil and gut feeling of how well the shot had gone . . . all this had trained him to know weapons and killing. He could not have missed this shot. He simply could not have.

Slocum opened the breech and looked inside, then pulled out the cylindrical magazine and looked at the solitary remaining round. A coldness filled him. The slug had been removed, replaced with a blob of wax to hold in the gunpowder in the cartridge. Someone had made sure Caleb Newcombe would be firing blanks from this rifle.

Slocum should have stuck with his trusty Colt and not used the captain's rifle. But he hadn't known and, from the expression on Caleb's face when he was shot, he had not known about his ammunition, either.

Slocum made his way back to where he had left Caleb, but the officer was gone. Rather than calling out to find his friend, he went to the spot where they had first sighted the phantoms coming uphill from the direction of the ocean. Pausing, Slocum checked his pocket watch and determined it was still almost a half hour till dawn. He wasn't too sure about the tides but thought one might still be coming in. He started to drop the rifle he had been carrying, then decided he ought to show it to Caleb as proof there were more than ghostly goings-on at the Presidio.

Scrambling down the hillside, he reached the stony beach. Waves of fog rolled in as surely as the ceaseless tide, obscuring the coast. Checking to be sure he was near the foot of the path taken by the seeming phantoms, Slocum walked slowly and examined the ground. The combination of rock and sand did not take well to footprints, but he rounded a bend in the coast to see a long stretch that emerged from the fog.

"Hey, stop!" he shouted as two men dressed as sailors pushed a longboat back into the surf from a protected area on the beach fifty feet away. One looked up at Slocum, said something to his partner, then both put their backs to shoving against the wooden boat, sliding it over rock and sand, getting it into the water. When it began to float, they jumped in and began rowing, each one taking an oar to speed their departure.

Slocum lifted the rifle, then remembered it had only a single blank round left. He dropped the weapon and drew his six-shooter. The range was a bit much for a handgun, but Slocum was a good shot and had incentive to stop them. He fired once, twice. A long brown splinter flew off the boat's side immediately behind the nearest sailor. But it didn't cause the two sailors to stop rowing. If anything, they picked up the pace, one calling cadence to keep them rowing in unison.

Taking more careful aim, Slocum was about ready to loose another round when he heard crunching in the sand behind him. He half turned and then was sent staggering by the blow that crashed into the back of his head. Trying to keep his feet took him into the surf. A wave broke and knocked him down into the water.

As he fell, he got off a shot at his attacker. He heard an angry curse but thought he had missed. Then a second blow knocked him senseless, leaving him to lift and float out to sea on the retreating wave.

4

Slocum sputtered and struggled in the choking saltwater, thrashing around until his hand hit a gritty patch. He spun about, facedown, and pushed downward with both hands and feet. He was sucked toward distant China by the retreating waves but scrambled and kicked and finally got himself parallel with the bottom, which sloped away fast into the depths of the Pacific. From here he managed to take a feeble stroke or two, and then was almost drowned when a new incoming wave broke over him.

He twisted and finally spat out enough water to keep his lungs from filling. He blinked hard to get the stinging saltwater from his eyes and then saw how he was being pulled farther and farther from shore. Slocum blew what air remained in his lungs outward, stroked powerfully and then started directly for the shoreline. It took only two more waves pulling inexorably at him to realize he wasn't strong enough to fight the powerful forces of the Pacific Ocean.

Changing tactics, he angled toward the shore. Arms burning with effort, lungs shrieking for a decent breath of fresh air, he made his way closer and closer until his hands again touched bottom. He kept swimming another few strokes and then dug his toes into the sandy beach as if he were trying to stand in stirrups. This shot him forward to belly-flop on the sand. For a frantic moment he thought a new wave would grip him and pull him back into the ocean's grasp, but the water broke around him and deposited seaweed atop him. Slocum summoned the remainder of his strength and fought forward another yard. At the end of his rope, he collapsed. If his attacker had come back to be sure he had finished the job, he would have found Slocum as weak as a kitten.

A few minutes' rest brought Slocum enough energy to finish crawling from the ocean. His boots were filled with water and his shirt and jeans were beginning to stiffen with salt as they partially dried. He was in no mood to strip them off and wring them out, although that might have saved him some discomfort later. All he wanted to do was gather his wits and figure out what to do next. Touching the spot on the side of his head where he had been hit sent new lances of pain into his brain.

"Damn," Slocum said, seeing how bloody his fingers were where he had touched the tender spot. Salt got into the wound and caused it to burn like fire. This as much as anything else kept Slocum from passing out. Bit by bit he regained strength enough to stand on unsteady feet. He hunted the beach until he found his dropped Colt Navy, then tucked it into a wet holster. The Colt was a decent six-shooter but any dirt in it required immediate attention or it might fail when he needed it most. With the dunking it had received in the waters of the Pacific, he knew it had to be taken apart completely, then cleaned, oiled and reassembled with great care.

Looking around, Slocum tried to find the tracks of the man who had hit him from behind. All he discovered was a long piece of rotted driftwood that had been used as a club to smash him in the head. Slocum stepped on it and it broke in half with a dull, wet snap. If this had been a dry piece of wood, his attacker would have killed him with the first blow. Slocum was lucky to have escaped serious injury.

He began climbing back to the Presidio, his gait shaky at first and then steadier as he regained his strength. By the time he reached the top of the hill, dawn was breaking. The gray fog glowed with an inner ghost light and then slowly burned off as the sun's rays focused more and more on the floating moisture. Slocum made his way to the HQ building, not sure where he would find Caleb Newcombe.

He'd started down the corridor toward the captain's office when a gruff voice called to him.

"He's in here. Got it set up as an infirmary, for the time being."

Slocum looked in the opposite direction and saw an army major motioning to him.

"You look like you got pulled through a knothole backward," the officer said. As Slocum got closer, he saw the major's corps insignia.

"You the post sawbones?"

"I pass for one," the man said. He might have been wearing an officer's uniform but he looked nothing like one. He had a two-day growth of gray stubble, his eyes were bloodshot and his potent breath told Slocum he had been on a real bender. The major saw Slocum's quick appraisal and said, "You're right about it all."

"A two-day drinking spree?"

"You got that wrong," the major said. "It was three. You ain't gonna insult me by thinkin' I could get this shitfaced in only two days. No sir, I been workin' hard at it."

"Where's Captain Newcombe?"

"He's in my office. No serious injury, but I'm not so sure I can say that about you." The major reached out and touched Slocum's wound with surprisingly gentle fingers. It still hurt like hell. "Get your ass onto that table and let me patch you up."

"I want to talk to Caleb first."

"Go on in. No waiting. Hell, men desert this damned post rather than risk being tended by Major Clarence Ardmore. At your service, sir." The major made a small bow that was supposed to be theatrical. It turned out to look more comical, since he could hardly stand. The last doctor in the world Slocum wanted working on him was this drunkard.

"John," called Caleb Newcombe from the back of the office. He sat in a corner, a six-gun resting on his lap. Either he or Ardmore had stripped off his jacket. To Slocum's surprise, the shirt beneath wasn't very blood-soaked at all. "Let him fix you up. Clarence might look to be so soused that he can't stand, but he can work wonders in any condition this side of unconsciousness."

"That's not too reassuring," Slocum said. "What happened to you? You're not hardly wounded, from the look of it."

"The bullet hit my hand, then grazed my belt buckle. That kept me from taking the slug in the belly. But the blood spurting all over made it look like I had finally bought myself a farm."

"Glad you're not too seriously injured," Slocum said. Caleb's left hand was heavily bandaged, but otherwise he looked to be in good shape. Slocum reached over and picked up the officer's uniform jacket. His belt buckle was misshapen, showing how close Caleb had come to getting his belly blown open by the rifle round. As he tossed the jacket and belt back onto the chair where they had been draped, Slocum began to weave about.

"Sit yourself down and let ole Doc Ardmore tend you. Here. Suck on this. I do." The major thrust a bottle of whiskey into Slocum's hand. Slocum took a long pull, and then the room really began to spin, in wild, crazy circles.

"That's mighty potent tarantula juice," Slocum said. His voice sounded as if it came from a thousand miles away.

"You oughta taste what they serve down at the Cobweb Palace. Now that's *real* firewater."

Slocum was distantly aware of pain in his neck and head, but it faded and eventually he found himself regaining a semblance of his usual sharpness. He reached up and touched a gauze patch plastered on the side of his head and was surprised that the pain was gone. The bottle of whiskey was still half full.

"I might be a drunk but I'm also a damn fine doctor," Major Ardmore said. "Hell, ain't no way I could do half the things I've done if I was sober."

"As you were, Major," Caleb said sharply. "We appreciate your fine work, but why don't you go sleep off the liquor."

"Why don't I hie my wobbly ass back down to the Barbary Coast and sample a bit of libation in each of those horrid deadfalls."

"You will not leave the post," Caleb said in his best command voice.

"Need supplies," Ardmore said, obviously funning the adjutant. "Never enough medicinal supplies."

"Let's get to your office, Captain," Slocum said, seeing that Caleb had missed the taunting tone in the doctor's words. Like so many drunks, Ardmore enjoyed a good fight, and had stupidly picked one with a sober man he had just bandaged.

"You are a disgrace to the uniform," Caleb said stiffly.

"Might be you're right. I'll take it off. I'll take it off and run naked across the parade grounds. A good idea." Ardmore took the whiskey and downed enough to kill a cow. It hardly affected him.

Caleb grumbled as he left, Slocum following slowly. The major saluted Slocum with the bottle as he left, grinning ear to ear.

"See what I have to deal with? He's a fine surgeon but his behavior is so . . ."

"Unmilitary," Slocum said. "That's the least of your worries."

"He wasn't joking. He's likely to take off like so many of the others. So far no officer has deserted, but it's only a matter of time."

"I meant you have other problems. Problems caused by someone who hasn't gone over the hill."

"What do you mean?"

"Who has access to your rifles?" Slocum pointed to the rack on the wall. He had left the rifle with the blank round back on the shore, forgetting about it until now.

"Only me," Caleb said, frowning. "Why?"

"There's no lock on the rack," Slocum said.

"No, why bother?" Caleb Newcombe looked more intently at Slocum now. "What are you getting at?"

"The reason you shot clean through the ghost was simple enough: You were shooting blanks. I picked up your rifle after you got hit in the hand and missed a couple more times. I checked the last round. The slug had been replaced by a blob of wax."

"Why would anyone replace my ammo?"

Slocum let the question hang in the air. It was obvious. Caleb was coming around to believing in phantoms because of his assured marksmanship and the way his bullets would have had to have killed anything of flesh and blood.

"Anyone could have come in while I was out."

"That's what I thought," Slocum said grimly. He took out his six-gun and began stripping it down. "You have gun oil and a rag or do I have to find the armory?"

"Here," Caleb said, fumbling about in the box under his rifle rack. The captain watched Slocum work on his Colt for a spell, then asked, "What's going on, John? I can't make heads nor tails of it."

"I've got my suspicions, but I need to nail down a fact or two before accusing anyone of anything. Because if I'm wrong, you'll have more than desertions on your hands—you'll have an outright mutiny."

"What do you want me to do?"

"Sit tight. That's not going to be easy. Pretend nothing's happening, that we never had a fight with the ghosts tonight. Watch your troops for any sign they might know more than they're letting on."

"My troops?" Caleb's bitterness echoed through the room. "I'll be lucky if they show up for inspection, much less salute me."

Slocum reassembled his Colt, loaded it and shoved it into its holster. He was drying out, but his boots needed a great deal more time before he could walk without making squishing sounds. Caleb saw this and silently went to a box next to his files and took out a pair of highly polished regulation cavalry trooper's boots. He handed them to Slocum.

"Those might fit. They have to be better than yours."

Slocum tried them on. They were a bit tight, but Caleb was right—they were better than trying to walk in his own waterlogged ones.

"Thanks. I'll be back when I can."

"Should I send a courier to Fort Point to bail you out again?"

"Won't be going in that direction now that the sun's burned off the damned fog." Slocum looked out the window onto a new day, one with patches of blue sky showing around the first rays of the rising sun. It was a perfect day for tracking down two murderous phantoms and the chained men they herded like animals.

Slocum made his way through the tight knots of blue-clad soldiers coming from their barracks, preparing for another day of garrison duty. At the edge of the parade grounds, Slocum got his bearings and went down the path to the cemetery. There he found the spent brass he had kicked from Caleb's rifle hours earlier, then walked directly for the spot in the trees where the ghost had mocked him before vanishing into the fog. With better visibility and a bright sun in his eyes, Slocum began casting about for the tracks that he was sure had been left.

To his chagrin, he couldn't find any. It was as if they *had* been phantoms. Slocum wasn't a particularly superstitious man, but the lack of footprints bothered him. He kept walking and soon found a well-worn path leading off the Presidio grounds and directly along the waterfront. He sucked in his breath.

The Barbary Coast. It might not have been the toughest, roughest section of any town he had ever seen, but it came close. Even Hell's Half Acre in Fort Worth couldn't hold a candle to the gangs, the crime, the outright debauchery of the Barbary Coast. It was just the kind of place he reckoned to find his answers.

The stench rising from streets filled with garbage was hardly diminished by a breeze picking up from the direction of San Francisco Bay that carried dead-fish odors with it. After he had walked down the streets for a spell, Slocum didn't even notice the stomach-turning reek. His quick eyes moved restlessly, taking notice of the men giving him an equally sharp look. Any show of weakness would make him prey. The area had been settled by the Sydney Ducks, an Australian gang that knew no rules but their own. They had been run out by even more formidable gangs.

"Hey, guy, want a bit of action?"

Slocum looked up to a second-story window. A soiled dove waggled her naked breasts in his direction, then turned and upended her skirt to give him an equally unobstructed view of her scrawny backside.

As he walked on without acknowledging her enticements, he heard her screeching about his lack of manhood.

Even over the deafening crescendo of the woman's shrieks, Slocum heard the scuffling of shoe soles on the cobblestones behind him. He spun to one side and thrust out his leg. His highly polished boot tripped a man trying to hit him with a cudgel. The man stumbled and fell to his knees, then froze when he felt the muzzle of Slocum's six-gun pressing into his temple.

"I'm looking for a couple gents dressed as soldiers," Slocum said.

"Try the fort, the one guarding the Golden Gate. Or up on the hill. The Presidio's got—" The would-be mugger flinched when Slocum cocked his six-shooter.

"The ones with the chained men. They come down here from the Presidio whenever there's a heavy fog. I want to talk to them."

"Don't know what you mean," the thug said. "I was jist walkin' along, mindin' my own business, and you attacked me."

"Remember harder," Slocum said, "or I might not leave you a whole lot to remember with."

"Go on, shoot me," the man said too loudly. "Go on, see if it gets you anywhere!"

This wasn't what Slocum had expected. Something was wrong; the man was trying to keep him distracted. Realizing this, Slocum kicked out and sent the man flopping face-down in the street as he swung around, six-shooter ready for action. The man's partner charged Slocum, a feral grin on his face as he lifted a long, rusty crowbar to bash in Slocum's skull.

Slocum never hesitated. His six-gun fired once, twice, a third time before the man decided to die.

Then Slocum found himself caught up in the middle of an even fiercer fight.

5

Slocum started to fire again at someone immediately behind the man with the crowbar. Only his quick reflexes saved the frightened red-haired woman.

"Duck!" he shouted. For an instant he thought the woman wasn't going to obey. Then she dropped like a stone and Slocum fired. His bullet parted the woman's hair across the top of her head, then lodged firmly in the chest of the man trying to grab her. Her attacker grunted, reached for the tiny red spot on his shirt and finally slumped. One down, two dead, but there was a steady stream of cutthroats pouring into the street now.

Slocum grabbed the woman's thin arm and pulled her erect.

"How many?"

"What?" she said stupidly.

"How many men are after you?"

She shook her head numbly as Slocum pulled her along behind him like a lamb on a rope. Then he spun her around into a doorway, turned and fired. This shot only winged the scarred, plug-ugly man rushing toward them. The nick on the thug's arm enraged him, forcing Slocum to fire again. This shot caught the man in his belly and doubled him over. Behind him came three more cutthroats swinging chains and wielding knives. Slocum thought fast and knew he was out of ammo.

Pushing away from the woman, who tried to grab him for protection, he kicked past her and knocked the flimsy door off its hinges. With a headlong rush, he carried her into the room he had just opened up, half dragging her behind as he made his way through what must have been a warehouse until he found another door, this one leading to a street running at right angles to the one he had just been on.

"Who are you?" the redhead gasped out. "You're gonna sell me to them, ain't ya?"

"I'm trying to get the hell out of here. You can stay or you can come with me." The thunder of running feet behind them in the warehouse convinced the woman. Better to be with one man she thought wanted to rape her than to be at the mercy of a dozen who wanted the same thing. When he saw her acquiesce, Slocum drew back the locking bar on the door and popped into the street. She followed on his heels, then watched as he jammed the locking bar under the door handle. It wouldn't do much more than slow the men chasing them, but every second counted.

He looked around. Nobody paid any attention to them; people being kidnapped or killed in the streets was pretty commonplace. Down the street Slocum saw a pair of San Francisco policemen sauntering along, swinging their billy clubs and looking like cocks-of-the-walk in their bright blue uniform jackets with shiny brass buttons in a double row down the front. He had little time for lawmen, but he needed allies against the gang coming after him.

"No, not them. Not them Specials. They'll sell us out fer sure." The woman's frightened voice told Slocum she wasn't leading him astray.

Slocum turned and put his arm around her waist, hurrying her along the street in the same direction as the two Specials. He took a side street the first chance he got, then urged the woman to break out in a dead run. She had a hard time keeping up. Her thin chest rose and fell heavily as she gasped for breath after only a few seconds of running. Slocum kept her going by reminding her what would happen if the gang caught her.

This added speed to her feet, but only for a few more seconds. Seeing that she was going to collapse, Slocum grabbed her arm and swung her about into an alley, where she sank gratefully to her hands and knees, sounding like a fireplace bellows as she struggled to regain her wind.

Slocum worked methodically to reload his six-shooter, sure that their pursuers would be on them in a flash. He snapped home the reloaded cylinder and felt a world better for it. Only then did he look at the woman, still on hands and knees in the alleyway, and wonder what the gang had wanted with her. She was obviously a whore, and not too attractive a one at that. She turned pale blue, bloodshot eyes up to him in thanks.

"You sure pulled my fat outta the fire," she said. "I kin do you here, if you like, to repay you."

"I've got other things in mind," he said. The flash of fear on her face told him they were talking at cross-purposes. "I'm looking for men dressed up in army uniforms."

"Get a lot of 'em from the post," the woman said. "My name's Lily. If you want, we kin go back to the house and do it there. In a clean bed 'n ever'thing. I'm real good. All the gents say so."

"Would you be safe at the brothel?" Slocum wasn't sure if that was the kind of "house" Lily meant, or if she worked out of some four-by-eight crib behind a deadfall.

"Oh, yes, Madame Lysette wouldn't let nuthin' happen to any of her ladies. She's real good to me and the rest."

"Where can we find Madame Lysette?"

Slocum watched warily as Lily led him back into the street. The men chasing the Cyprian had vanished as surely as the fog had that morning. Still, Slocum kept one hand on the ebony butt of his six-shooter and felt he needed eyes in the back of his head to keep from getting waylaid again. Lily's mood had changed radically. She was downright cheerful now, laughing and waving to people in the street, even making suggestions as lewd as the one the whore in the second-story window had. Heading south, they came to Fulton Street. Lily hesitated, as if she wasn't sure what to do.

"My mistress, Madame Lysette, she don't like nobody bringin' uninvited guests back. She runs a real high-class place."

"I'll square it with her," Slocum said. Lily looked at what had been highly polished boots. Slocum could almost hear the wheels grinding in the fragile whore's head, estimating the cost of the boots and taking in the way Slocum had acquitted himself in the middle of the Barbary Coast.

"You will? I wasn't supposed to be out like I was. I mean, I got me a steady boyfriend along the docks. He works as a barkeep, and Madame Lysette don't 'low none of her fancy ladies to go fraternizin' with such low characters."

"I'll talk to her," Slocum assured the redhead.

"Then I'll do you good. I'll make sure you never fergit Lily and how good she was to you."

Slocum let her lead the way to a luxurious house sandwiched between two larger buildings at either end of the block on Bush Street. The grounds were well kept and the house was in good repair. Madame Lysette's business had to be profitable.

"There you are, you naughty girl," said a handsome older woman opening the front door as Slocum and Lily went up the slate walk. "You shouldn't go off unescorted, Miss Lily. It's not right." The steel edge to the madam's voice made Lily cringe. The redhead turned and pointed at Slocum.

"He'll vouch for me. Go on, tell her." Lily struggled for his name, but he had never given it.

Slocum removed his hat and nodded in Madame Lysette's direction.

"Ma'am, my name's John Slocum. I happened on this young lady, who happened to need an escort home. I was happy to oblige." Slocum put his hat back on and started to go. He had no business here and certainly wanted nothing from Lily. If he spent too much time with her, he'd get more than trouble.

"Wait a moment, sir," Madame Lysette called. She frowned a moment, then smiled as she looked him over. "I see you are a gentleman. A Southern gentleman, if I hear the accent. Alabama?"

"Georgia," Slocum said.

"Do come in and allow me to give you something to take the edge off your thirst." Her nose wrinkled slightly. "You might want to wash up, also. The odor of . . . gunpowder is strong."

"There was a lot of shootin', Madame Lysette," Lily said. "He saved my life, he did!"

"You run up to your room. You'll be late for your first . . . appointment."

"Right away," Lily said. When she reached the doorway behind Madame Lysette, she made a lewd gesture to Slocum, then pointed upstairs and mouthed "One hour."

It would be a cold day in hell before Slocum shared a bed with her.

"It was good of you to make certain Lily got back safely. What was the nature of her rescue?"

"A gang of men attacked her. She said she was in the Barbary Coast to visit a boyfriend who worked as a bartender there."

"What do *you* think?" Madame Lysette's voice was soft, but her gray eyes were as cold as the Pacific Ocean.

"She got turned around," Slocum said. "She was in Chinatown and wandered out of an opium den, got confused where she was and looked like easy pickings for the desperados there."

"A Southern gentleman, and one who sees the world as it is. Lily has used the story of a boyfriend once too often, I fear. I must confine her to her quarters until she is over her craving for opium."

"Won't be pretty," Slocum said.

"Of course not, but Lily is useless to me as long as she is a slave to such a vile drug. You saw her condition. She was once a sweet, svelte young woman who had men lined up around the block demanding her favors."

"At a dollar a tumble," Slocum said.

"Not quite that much, but if she had applied herself, she might have earned such a princely sum. Yes, you are a real find, Mr. Slocum. Straightforward, honest, nothing gets by you. And from the look of your weapon, you are accustomed to desperate situations. Why were you in the Barbary Coast? Especially, why were you there wearing someone else's boots?"

Slocum didn't have any reason to confide in the madam and didn't, but he followed her into a well-appointed parlor and sat in a velvet-covered plush chair. Everything about the house and the woman shouted "Money!" He was beginning to wonder what she wanted from him.

"I ran afoul of some gamblers," Slocum said, wary of divulging too much about his mission for Caleb Newcombe. He decided to stick with something that was also the truth, and that required less explanation. "Let's say it was all a misunderstanding."

"Indeed, you have the look of a man who would never get into such a circumstance."

"My partner got into a game and didn't know who the sucker was. He anted up his life, but that wasn't enough. The other tinhorns in the game reckoned they could collect what they said he lost to them."

"They're quite wrong, of course. If they try to push

you too much, they will end up dead. Is that why you were going . . . hunting?"

"I was taking in the fine sea air," Slocum said, tiring of the politeness covering Madame Lysette's real intentions. "What do you want from me?"

"A trade, perhaps. I find myself in a peculiar position. My concierge has, shall we say, become indisposed."

"Your bouncer?"

"Oh, Pierre is far more than that. He is an able manager, plays a fine piano and often escorts me to the fancy dress balls. However Pierre is incapacitated after a misunderstanding with some very powerful men in this city."

"I want to know what happened to him, so it won't happen to me also," said Slocum. He watched the woman's reaction. Madame Lysette hesitated, then came to a conclusion.

"The truth is, I don't know exactly what happened. Pierre was entering the rear of the house when someone shot him from ambush. He took a bullet in the thigh and another in his . . . Well, let's say he is inconvenienced when he sits down. His recovery will take a week or more before he can walk, much less do what is required of my employee for this particular undertaking."

"I don't follow you," said Slocum.

"These gamblers who are troubling you—do they have names?"

"Gabe Walensky, his brother Herk, and another bottom-dealer I don't know."

"I do. Big Pete Ordway. He fancies himself to be quite the bare-knuckles brawler. In return for a favor which you seem admirably capable of performing, I will see that these most annoying gamblers do not trouble you again, Mr. Slocum. Are you agreeable to such a deal?"

"Depends," answered Slocum. "What do I have to do? Kill someone?" He saw Madame Lysette's carefully plucked eyebrows arch ever so slightly. Then she laughed.

"Why, good heavens, no! Nothing so crude, sir. Besides, if I wanted someone killed, that would be no problem. No, Mr. Slocum, I want you to escort me to the Mayor's Fancy Dress Ball this evening."

Slocum thought he had heard it all. He was wrong. He sat speechless for a moment, then found himself nodding agreement.

6

Slocum felt funny gussied up in the monkey suit, but he was no stranger to such sartorial finery. In fact, the last time he had been dressed in a cutaway coat had been here in San Francisco over two years ago, when he had been on a hot streak and was gambling at a private club atop Russian Hill. He studied himself critically in a full-length mirror, and patted down the wine-colored brocade vest a mite to get rid of wrinkles caused by the derringer tucked into a small pocket where he could fish it out in a hurry. Slocum wasn't sure what kind of shindig Madame Lysette was dragging him to, but he wanted to be prepared.

What didn't seem right to him was taking money from the woman to pay off his partner's gambling debt. The gamblers were lowlifes who had no call demanding that Slocum pony up money lost by someone else, especially since Slocum hadn't been there and thought the Walenskys and their partner, Big Pete, had probably cheated. Why Madame Lysette should pay them rather than Slocum, even given his so-called service this evening, was a moral dilemma he wrestled with.

"Ah, Mr. Slocum, you do clean up well," came a lilting voice from the doorway of the small bedroom where

51

Slocum had found the clothing and had dressed. He shifted slightly and saw Madame Lysette perfectly framed by the wood doorway. Her strawberry blonde hair was done up in a swirl dotted with sparkling gems and small opalescent orbs. Slocum didn't have to ask if they were real diamonds and pearls. Somehow, he doubted this woman spared any expense when it came to image.

Her dress was long, flowing and of a claret color matching his vest. Gathered cunningly here and there, the evening gown revealed the swell of her breasts perfectly and even hinted at the slender ankles beneath the floor-length skirt. She held a small fan that might have been carved from ivory. Seeing his intent examination, she smiled just a little, opened the fan and pretended to look at him coyly.

"I do declare, are you staring at me, Mr. Slocum? Whatever should a lady think of such rude behavior?"

"You should think I'm appreciative of your beauty," he said. "That's a mighty fine dress, but I suspect you'd look even finer without it."

"Now, Mr. Slocum, don't mix business and pleasure."

"Which is which?"

For a moment, he saw a flare of anger in her gray eyes. When she lowered her fan, the smile was still intact, but the tone had turned chilly.

"Tonight, sir, is business. This evening you are to escort me, to say little unless required and to attend me."

"Like Pierre would have," he said.

"I am glad you understand. The carriage is waiting." She spun, her skirts swirling as she flounced off for the front room, where her shawl lay draped over a chair. Slocum followed, saw she waited for him, and graciously slipped it around her shoulders. This action mollified her some, but Slocum saw that Madame Lysette was not pleased with his reaction. He wondered if she had expected him to be slavishly grateful for offering to remove Walensky, his overfed brother and their partner from his trail.

She favored him with a small nod of her head, then waited for him to extend his arm. Slocum escorted the madam to the door, opened it and led her out to the waiting carriage. He tried not to show his surprise at the elegance of the carriage, with its silver trim and what looked to be a coat of arms on its side.

They rattled through the gaslit streets, heading for Ralston's elegant Palace Hotel. From the corner of his eye, Slocum studied Madame Lysette as they rode, but the woman said nothing. Her eyes remained fixed outside the carriage—watching what, Slocum could not tell. From the intense expression on her face, she might be plotting and planning everything she would say and do throughout the evening. He had already figured out this was not a social event for her. It was nothing less than a business meeting though with everyone in formal dress. He wasn't sure why she had offered him this deal, but there had to be a reason. Nothing the blonde woman did was without purpose.

The carriage came to a smooth halt, and footmen leaped to help Madame Lysette down. Slocum followed, barely noticed. That suited him just fine. This wasn't his kind of place. If he had to choose, he would have preferred to be in the Cobweb Palace tottering at the end of a pier in the Barbary Coast than at the Palace Hotel, would have rather been rubbing elbows with drunks and gamblers than with San Francisco's high society. He paused inside the door and looked around the foyer. To the left, under glittering crystal chandeliers, stretched the enormous ballroom. Strains of a waltz drifted out and through the door, where Slocum saw couples spinning to the airs. As he and Madame Lysette got to the door, Slocum's estimation sagged. The dancers looked intent, intense, too concentrated on behaving properly to ever enjoy the dance. They needed to get the band to strike up a Virginia reel and abandon all pretense of sobriety.

With that in mind, Slocum looked around. All he saw

was a solitary punch bowl at the far side of the ballroom, presided over by a liveried servant.

"One or two drinks only," Lysette cautioned. "I will not tolerate drunkenness."

"I wouldn't think of it," Slocum said, getting a hot look from the woman. "I need only look at you to become completely intoxicated with your beauty."

"You do go on, even for a Georgia gentleman," Madame Lysette said, smiling genuinely for the first time. "Don't stop. I like it."

Slocum had no chance to say anything more, as two expensively dressed, portly men came over and paid their respects to Lysette. Slocum saw how one of them eyed him. Slocum was enough of a poker player to read the man's mind: He wondered what Slocum was to Madame Lysette. The man didn't dismiss him out of hand—quite—but the expression told Slocum that he wanted to.

"Mr. Slocum, please meet the mayor of San Francisco. Mr. Mayor, this is my . . . good friend, John Slocum."

"Pleased to meet you," said the man who had been evaluating Slocum. He shook hands, but his grip was flaccid and clammy in Slocum's hard hand. Whatever the mayor had done before being elected, it had nothing to do with real work. "If you'll excuse me, I must talk with some important constituents," the mayor said, bowing slightly to Lysette. Slocum saw the look that passed between them, then saw an older woman a few paces away looking daggers at the mayor.

"Yes, do get on about your business, Mr. Mayor. Mr. Slocum wants to dance, anyway. Good evening, sir."

The mayor and the man with him hurried off to greet others coming in.

"The mayor's wife?" Slocum put his arm out, and as Madame Lysette took it, he steered her about for a good look.

"Why, yes, I believe it is," the strawberry blonde said

easily. "She does not understand how her husband is in such demand, even at such a festive gala."

She paused, turned to face him and then said, "You can dance, can't you, John?"

Slocum slipped his arm around her waist and spun her onto the floor. It took a few seconds for him to fall into the rhythm of the waltz, but from Madame Lysette's expression she was pleasantly surprised at his expertise. At the end of the dance, she used her fan to cool herself.

"My, that was most strenuous," she said. "And you did not step on my feet once."

"And you didn't step on mine, either, but then I'm used to dodging cows so they don't crush my feet."

For a moment, Madame Lysette looked at him with wide gray eyes, then she laughed.

"You are a continual surprise, John. I may have misjudged you."

"But you have business to attend to and will leave me to my own devices," Slocum said.

"I *did* underestimate you. Go, find the bar and get some decent liquor. Ask for the special stock, not that rotgut they try to pass off as fine French champagne. They do have a few cases of Monopole about, I am sure, since it is Mr. Ralston's favorite."

Madame Lysette fanned herself vigorously for a moment, gave him a sultry look over the top of the ivory fan, then glided away, greeting the men in a small group to one side of the dance floor. Slocum guessed these were the politicians who ran San Francisco from the way they dressed and acted. There might have been more than one millionaire in the lot, too, from the eye-dazzling gleam of diamond studs and headlight diamond stickpins in wide satin lapels.

Slocum saw that she was going to be occupied with these men for some time, so he took her advice to find the bar. To his relief, the punch bowl was only for those who wanted to delicately sip and pretend that demon rum never passed their lips. Behind the bowl was a partially open door leading to the bar, where men smoked and drank decent whiskey. Slocum ordered a bourbon and was pleasantly surprised to get the real thing, not the alcohol laced with rusty nails and gunpowder that comprised the trade whiskey Slocum was usually forced to drink.

"Damned animals, that's what they are," said a man with a walrus mustache next to Slocum at the bar. "The lot of them should be shipped back to their filthy country."

Slocum hesitated, wondering what the man was talking about. The tall, whipcord-thin man with him nodded in agreement. "The Celestials have to be kept in their place. Sojourners, that's all they are. No pride in this country."

"Look at how they live," said the first man, twirling the tip of his bushy mustache. "The Cubic Air Ordinance won't stop them from crowding a dozen to a room to live. We need something more."

"A hunt," said the thinner man, laughing. "That's what we need. A hunt. Hounds after them, like they were nothing but foxes."

Slocum drifted away as the men began spinning wild tales of chasing Chinese men up and down the streets of Chinatown behind a pack of dogs while riding fine steeds. Slocum needed another drink to take the bad taste out of his mouth. Somehow, it didn't go down as good as the first had. As he turned from the bar, he saw the mayor and Madame Lysette talking intimately. She leaned over and kissed his ear, then reached down low and squeezed, causing the politician to jump.

Slocum wondered what he was supposed to do when the mayor and Lysette made their way along the wall of the ballroom, reached a small door some distance off and vanished through it. Slocum started to follow, then saw the mayor's wife standing to one side, looking vexed.

He went to her, bowed slightly and said, "May I have this dance?"

"Why, I . . . Yes, of course, sir," the woman said. "I don't believe I've seen you at any of these dreadful affairs before."

"I just arrived in town," Slocum said, "and will be leaving soon."

"A pity." The woman fit well in his arms as they spun to the music. Not unexpectedly, the woman was a far better dancer than Slocum, but she didn't take notice of his small hesitations as they danced.

"You aren't a business partner of my husband, are you?" she asked suspiciously.

"I'm not even sure what business your husband is in," Slocum said honestly. "I came with someone who seems to have . . . left."

"She's a fool." The woman snorted in contempt. "But then, my husband's a fool, too."

Slocum had begun the dance out of duty to Madame Lysette, thinking it was his job to occupy the mayor's wife while the madam occupied the mayor. As they danced, Slocum saw the mayor's assistant looking daggers at him from the side of the ballroom.

"Who's that?" Slocum asked.

"Oh, ignore him. That's Claude Gorham, my husband's administrative assistant. He can be such a bore."

"He's gesturing to you. Perhaps it's something important."

"Oh, you're right. Though it could not be very important—not as important as another dance with you, sir," the woman said, smiling almost shyly. "But I'll see what he wants."

Slocum remained where he stood while the mayor's wife went to see what had so agitated Gorham. It didn't come as much of a surprise when Claude Gorham pushed past the woman and came directly over to Slocum, leaving her behind.

"Your presence is no longer required, sir," Gorham said in what he thought was a menacing tone. Slocum almost laughed in the short, pudgy man's face.

"That's not for you to say."

"She wants you to leave."

" 'She'? The mayor's wife?" Slocum had to smile at the way the man's face turned red with poorly suppressed anger.

"You know whom I mean. Her. *Her!*"

"I'd like to speak to her myself, just to be sure the messenger boy didn't get confused." Slocum made no effort to hide the contempt in his voice. Claude Gorham sputtered, then pointed.

"Out there."

It wasn't the door taken by Madame Lysette and her paramour the mayor, but Slocum nodded curtly, then went to the door. As he passed through into a short corridor beyond, he heard voices ahead. Curious, he lengthened his stride and went down the fifteen feet to an outer door.

"Lysette?" As he stepped outside, both his arms were seized in viselike grips. Slocum jerked about, trying to escape, but a third man joined the fray and swung a blackjack that clipped him just above the ear. All strength flooded from his body as he sagged in the grips of the two men. In the far distance, past the roaring in his ears, Slocum heard the man who had sapped him order the other two to get rid of him.

He fought to get his feet under him, but his legs refused to obey.

"What'll we do with 'im?" asked one of the men.

"I got an idea."

Slocum heard the men chuckling as they pulled him behind them, the tops of his once-polished shoes dragging along the lawn and then the dirt as they took him to the stables, then flopped him belly-down over a horse. Two quick turns of a rope bound Slocum's wrists and secured him as they led the horse from the stall.

Slocum's head felt as if it would split open by the time they'd gotten some distance away from the Palace Hotel. He began struggling against the ropes holding his wrists, but the strength was still missing from his limbs. He felt the lump of the derringer pressing into his chest, but with his hands bound as they were, he could not hope to reach the small weapon. Besides, Slocum feared his numbness would cause him to fumble the gun and lose all chance at getting revenge on the two men.

"Here," one called. "This is a good place."

Slocum felt one rope being loosened. He slid from the horse and fell in a pile in the dusty street, half propped against a building.

"Go on, do it," urged the second man.

Slocum shook his head; a hive of angry bees buzzed about. He reached up and felt the tender spot where he had been hit. His fingers came away sticky with his own blood for the second time in as many days. This sent a surge of anger through him that pushed aside the muzziness and fed strength to his arms and legs. He began testing his wrists and felt enough slack in the rope to let him twist free. As the rope fell away and he reached hesitantly for the derringer hidden in his vest pocket, he heard one man shouting, "I hate all you damn Chinks! You slant-eyed sons of bitches oughta be sent back to where you come from!" The curses became even more vitriolic as they were directed at ancient Chinese ancestors, echoing down the deserted street into the distance for everyone to hear. Then the string of curses stopped as quickly as it had begun.

Slocum blinked hard and got his vision cleared enough to see three horses trotting away; two had riders and the third must have been the one he had been draped over to arrive at this sorry pass.

He forced himself to stand, and his legs almost betrayed him. Leaning heavily against the wall, he waited for the spinning to stop and his legs to firm.

Like the ghosts plaguing the Presidio, dark forms were moving within shadows along the street. Coming for him.

He raised his hand to hold them at bay, to give himself time to explain what had happened. Slocum jerked away when he heard a whistling sound followed by a *thud!* A hatchet was buried into the wall beside him.

Claude Gorham's henchmen had brought Slocum to Chinatown and then made sure they attracted unwanted attention to him.

"Wait, I can explain," Slocum got out before he had to duck another thrown hatchet. There was no arguing with the highbinders coming after him, all believing he had shouted the curses, defaming them and their ancestors.

7

Slocum bent low, tore the vest pocket open as he grabbed for the derringer hidden there, then brought up the two-shot pistol, looking for a Chinese target. The street was empty again. But the feeling of being watched told Slocum he was anything but alone. He was surrounded by men carrying more of the vicious sharp-bladed hatchets, like the pair stuck in the wall beside his head.

He pried loose one of the hatchets, knowing it would come in handy later when he ran out of bullets. Two shots didn't amount to a hill of beans when he was up against a small army of Celestials intent on parting his hair right down the middle with a razor-sharp blade. More out of instinct than because he heard anything, Slocum went into a gunfighter's crouch and pointed the small pistol to his right. His finger drew back smoothly. The tiny *pop!* was followed by a grunt. The pellet of lead had winged one of the highbinders, but Slocum never saw the man; he had faded back into shadow too quickly.

A quick step in that direction to follow the wounded man brought a flurry of sound from behind. Slocum glanced over his shoulder and caught sight of a mountain of a Chinaman rushing him. He tried to swing back and fire, but powerful hands shoved him hard enough to ruin his aim. He hit the ground and his derringer went flying, to discharge when it smashed into a brick wall. It was of no more use to him anyway, because he had fired the two rounds. Slocum brought up the hatchet he had pulled from the wall, only to have it brushed aside with contemptuous ease.

"I thought you fellows were supposed to be small," Slocum said to the huge man towering above him. The man grinned, showing a broken front tooth, then reached for Slocum. Twisting hard, Slocum kicked out, his foot crashing into the man's kneecap at the same time he locked his other foot behind a thick ankle.

For a heart-pounding moment Slocum thought nothing was going to happen. Then the man yelped and tumbled back, a felled giant tree in a forest of smaller saplings.

Slocum jumped to his feet and found himself surrounded by a ring of men more in keeping with his image of Celestials. None came to his shoulder and all wore the stereotype curious padded jackets, baggy trousers and slippers. What Slocum also noted were the wickedly long knives and deadly hatchets they wielded with obvious expertise.

"I've got no fight with you," he said. Slocum had heard of Chinese gangs—tongs—and knew they were as brutal as the Sydney Ducks had ever been. "The men with me shouted all those insults." He looked around the ring of impassive faces and ebony-dark eyes and knew they either didn't understand or, more likely, didn't care. They wanted his blood, and nothing was going to stop them.

When one took a sliding step toward him, Slocum clumsily swung the hatchet he had retrieved, intending to do nothing more than hold the man at bay while he thought up better arguments to keep the group from killing him. The Celestial parried the slow attack with his knife, and then swarmed in with startling speed.

Slocum was bent double as a bony fist crashed into his

belly. The few times he had felt this much pain had been in bare-knuckle fights with Irishmen twice the size of the Celestial. Now, the blows came faster than he could see them and landed on nerves that made him want to scream and retch and pass out all at once.

Slammed back against the wall, Slocum managed to get his knee lifted so he could kick out and get the man away from him. The punishment had only begun, however. The man bounced away like a child's ball, leaving room for two others to rush Slocum. He swung his hatchet with as much strength as he could muster, but he was still weakened by the blackjack blow to the head that had allowed Claude Gorham's henchmen to abandon him in Chinatown.

Dropping the hatchet, Slocum grabbed the man to his left in a bear hug, trying to use the Celestial's body as a shield against the others' attacks. It didn't work. He found himself hanging on to a tornado that whirled about in the circle of his arms, inflicting painful punishment to every exposed portion of Slocum's anatomy. With a heave, Slocum threw the man into the arms of two others and stumbled away, the wall protecting his left side.

He had sown some confusion, but not enough. Slocum heard a whirring sound, then felt his legs go out from under him. He crashed forward to the street and then everything went black momentarily as another blow to his head knocked him flat when he tried to scramble away.

Strong hands pulled him to his feet and a blindfold wrapped itself around his aching head.

"Walk. Or die."

Slocum wasn't too surprised that at least one of the Chinese spoke English well enough to bark out this order. But the Celestials' expertise ended there. Slocum was able to peer past the edge of the filthy rag tied over his eyes to see where they were taking him. First they spun him around in circles a few times to make sure he was disoriented, then they shoved him toward the door in the very building whose wall he had used to make his stand. The door opened to a pitch-black interior, but they quickly turned him and went downstairs into a basement.

Or so Slocum thought until he saw a flicker of light from a lantern up ahead. They were leading him into the tunnels beneath Chinatown. His shoulders brushed both walls of the narrow tunnel as they took one turn after another. Although Slocum saw where he was going, the constant turning confused him. He might as well have been completely blindfolded for all the good it did him trying to remember the route.

"There." A strong hand shoved him to his knees, and they began the beating. No single blow was hard enough to disable him, but the bony fists came in a torrential outpouring of hatred that he could not defend against. Slocum curled up and let them hit and kick him. Somehow the punches were weaker than the kicks, so he struggled to get to a spot where they could only beat him with their hands.

This went on for a nightmarishly long time, then hands seized him and flung him into a rickety chair. Before he could raise his leaden arms, his wrists were secured behind him, then fastened to the chair. His ankles were similarly tied to the front legs of the chair.

"What do you want from me?"

The only answer Slocum got was a hard blow to the face that rocked him, as some of them made sure he didn't turn the chair over and escape the punishment descending upon him with relentless fury.

A singsong command went out, and the beating stopped. Slocum could hardly hear for the surflike roar of blood in his ears. His face felt twice its normal size, and there wasn't a muscle in his body that hadn't been brutalized.

"You will tell him to stop it."

"What're you talking about? Tell who? Tell him what?" Slocum gasped as a powerful blow to his belly took the wind from him.

More quick Chinese words were exchanged. Slocum guessed there were as many as half a dozen men in the room. When he tipped his head to one side and peered past the blindfold, he caught sight of three. One was the mountain of a man he had fought out in the street. The giant limped a little, telling Slocum he had inflicted some small damage. This was cold comfort, knowing he wasn't going to leave the room alive.

"We leave you for rats to eat. For a while. If you do not cooperate then, we will kill you."

"Who are you talking about? What am I supposed to tell him?"

"Your boss. You know what we want."

"Wait!" Slocum heard the Chinese shuffle from the room, leaving him alone with his thoughts and the distant scurrying of rats coming to investigate what might be a decent meal for a change. Fresh meat. His flesh.

Slocum strained and tried to loosen a leg or a rung in the chair, but it proved sturdier than he had expected. Or perhaps he was far weaker than he thought. Try as he might, he could make no headway against the ropes cutting cruelly into his wrists and ankles.

In the distance he heard the singsong argument going on. He knew by its tone that he was in a heap of trouble. When they decided he didn't know who this "boss" was or what to tell him, they would kill him out of hand. They hadn't shown any mercy so far, and Slocum doubted they would ever consider that they had nabbed an innocent bystander.

Or as innocent as he could be.

His nose twitched when a different scent reached his nostrils. It took a few seconds for him to identify this odor that was so out of place in the stench of the cellar. Jasmine. He wondered if the Chinese were burning joss sticks. Then he heard a furtive sound behind him and felt feathery touches on his arms.

"Who's there?" he asked.

"Shush," came the whispered reply. "You must run fast. Leave before they return."

"Easier said than done," he said, craning around and trying to peer at the woman who wore the jasmine perfume. He winced as a knife sliced both rope and wrist.

"So sorry," she said as she worked on his other bonds. For a moment Slocum wondered if his circulation would ever return, then he worried he would never be able to use his fingers again, they felt so fat and full of pain.

"Oh!"

"What is it?" Slocum ripped off the blindfold and looked around, but the woman had run off. On the floor lay a small jade knife, almost a letter opener rather than a serious weapon; but it had cut his ropes. Slocum picked it up, used it on the remaining strands holding his feet and stood on shaky legs.

He heard the argument winding down and knew he had very little time to take his mysterious rescuer's advice and get the hell out of this rabbit warren under the streets of Chinatown. From the brief glimpses he'd had on his way to this filthy, cramped, rat-filled room, he knew he had to go back past the highbinders who were deciding his fate. Slocum went to the doorway and chanced a quick glance and saw the highbinders gathered in a small circle near a lantern. They passed a cigarette around. Each took a puff before handing it to the man on his left. This occupied them for the moment, but Slocum knew that when the smoke was finished, they would reach their decision.

He also knew it wouldn't be favorable to him, since he couldn't give them what they wanted. He wasted no time backtracking to the center of the room and looking for some other way out of the rat's maze of tunnels. Only one option presented itself.

Slocum took off through the tunnel his mysterious benefactor had taken, though he'd seen neither her nor anyone else in the tunnel when he spotted a rusty iron grating in the roof. Curiosity about the woman's identity took second place to self-preservation. Slocum used the small jade knife to pry out the grating and then boosted himself up and out onto the street. To his surprise it was still dark, maybe an hour before sunrise.

He got his bearings and headed for the Presidio, vengeance burning bright in him.

8

"Halt and be recognized!"

Slocum limped a few more paces and obeyed. The climb up the hill to the front gate of the Presidio had taken what little energy he had left.

"What you want?" demanded the guard, coming out from his post with a rifle leveled at Slocum.

"Want to see Captain Newcombe," Slocum said.

"You're . . . Why, man alive! You're Mr. Slocum!"

"Reckon so." Slocum wobbled on his feet and wondered if there was a square inch of his body that hadn't been pummeled and bruised to the point of destruction. He had a powerful lot of revenge to catch up on. First, though, a bath, a good meal and a day's sleep. Then he would consider what had to be done.

"It's me, Private Carpenter. Leonard Carpenter."

Slocum remembered him from their discussion in the mess, although he hadn't gotten the stripling's name then. The mess hall sergeant, Kendricks, had been there to give the private coffee laced with whiskey to loosen up his observations about the phantoms wandering the Presidio. Slocum was glad that someone who knew him was manning the sentry point. It saved having to answer a lot of questions he wasn't up to answering.

"You see any more haints?"

"No, sir, not this night. But then, there ain't been a whole lot of fog, bein' kinda windy and all. Never see 'em 'less there's heavy fog. Then the rattlin' chains and—"

"Private, could you help me to my quarters? I'm a bit tuckered out. It's been a rough night."

"Yes, sir. I do declare. You look like you really tied one on." Private Carpenter canted his head to one side as he studied Slocum more closely. "Truth is, looks like somebody's been whalin' the livin' tar outta you."

"A little of both," Slocum admitted.

"Uh, sir, I got orders 'bout you. To take you direct to the captain's office."

"I suppose he wants to talk to me about the phantoms," Slocum said.

"The captain don't confide in me. He ain't there right now, but you're supposed to wait in his office till he does show up."

Slocum heaved a deep sigh and felt the pain lacing throughout his body. He might have a cracked rib, but it probably hadn't been broken. If it had, there'd be white bone poking through his skin by now after all the punishment he'd taken.

"I need a bath before I talk to the captain," Slocum said. "I'll get to my quarters and clean myself up, then go wait for him."

"Well, if you say so, sir." Private Carpenter was obviously tossed on the horns of a dilemma. His commanding officer had told him one thing; now a civilian was telling him something else. Who was the superior?

"Anyone around you might tell that I'm back?" Slocum didn't add "anyone who'd give two good goddamns," though he realized that only Caleb Newcombe was likely to care that he had returned.

"I'll send word, sir."

Slocum did the best he could to walk straight and proud, but every step cost him that much more of his jealously hoarded strength. By the time he reached the visitors' quarters Caleb had assigned him to, he was about ready to flop on the bunk and forget about a bath. His time in the CSA Army had taught him the value of sleep. It had also taught him how quickly disease spread. He stripped off his tattered fancy tuxedo and scuffed shoes, made his way to the end of the corridor and sat on a stone ledge, staring at the galvanized tub in the middle of the room. The Presidio had decent quarters for visiting dignitaries, he saw. There were pipes running out, and one delivered hot water to the tub. If only he could force himself that far.

"You are a sight," came a low voice. Slocum reached for his six-shooter, then realized he had left it back in Madame Lysette's brothel. He had also lost the derringer. But none of this mattered, since he was buck naked. He turned and saw Glory Newcombe standing in the doorway to the room, a fluffy towel draped over her arm.

"More than usual, I suspect," Slocum said. He was too battered and beaten to show any modesty. From the way the woman's eyes devoured every inch of his nakedness, she wasn't too shy and wasn't seeing anything she hadn't already. In some back corner of his mind Slocum wondered what her brother would think. Then it just didn't matter to him.

Glory went to the tub and twisted the faucet hard, getting the hot water flowing until steam began filling the room.

"That's going to scald the hide right off me," Slocum said. He could hardly see the woman through the clouds of steam billowing up to fill the small room.

"It feels fine to me. Come along now, John. You mustn't let it get cold."

Making his way through the steamy room, he put both hands on the edge of the tub for support. His eyes widened when he saw Glory. She had stripped off her own clothing and sat as naked as a jaybird in the tub. Slocum blinked moisture from his eyes to be sure he was seeing what he thought he saw. Glory sprawled back in the tub, her slender legs hiked up to either side. The water rose around her sleek body and only slowly hid the fleecy triangle between her white thighs.

"The water feels just about right," she said in a sultry voice. "The only way it'll be better is if you join me."

"I'm not up for what you're proposing," Slocum said. "I've been coldcocked and beaten and barely escaped with my life tonight."

"Coldcocked? I doubt that," Glory said, reaching out and running feverish fingers across his private parts. As her fingers curled around him, he felt stirrings he hadn't believed possible in his condition. "Get in, John. Get in and I'll . . . tend you real good."

She guided him around to sit facing away from her, snuggled between her long legs. She drew up her knees on either side of his body as he leaned forward slightly, then began washing his back. The warm water trickled down his spine and soothed, even as her probing fingers aroused him.

"You must have fought an army tonight," she said. "So many bruises. Let me kiss them and make them well."

Slocum tensed at first, then relaxed when her lips brushed over his flesh with teasing, fleeting kisses. Her soapy hands began working on areas other than his back, gently stroking down his battered ribs and then working around him, across his chest, his belly, lower.

"My, my, what have we here?" Glory asked in mock surprise. Her fingers closed around his meaty shaft and began working up and down slowly. Every trip to the very tip sent a new tremor of desire coursing into Slocum's body. The hot water and gentle laving had eased his aches and pains, but now a new tension was intruding. A pleasant one.

"Be sure you get it real clean."

"It's certainly hard. How would you suggest I scrub it? Perhaps I ought to lick it clean, like a cat?"

"Not if you have a rough tongue," Slocum said. "That's about the only part of me that hasn't been scraped raw or bruised."

"Oh, I promise not to hurt it any." Glory's fingers slipped away from the meaty stalk and dipped lower in the water, cradling the sac holding his family jewels. Her massaging made him even stiffer and caused Slocum to lift a bit out of the water, forcing him back involuntarily. He felt her firm, full breasts crushing against his back even as the hard nubs capping them pulsed with desire. This brought a soft moan of delight from the brunette and told Slocum she was enjoying this as much as he was.

He turned around and kissed her clumsily. Water sloshed out of the tub onto the tile floor, but neither noticed.

"Not that way," she said. Glory rose to her knees so that her chest was level with his face. Slocum never hesitated. He buried his face between those silken pillows and licked and kissed and nipped lightly at the succulent flesh he found. He licked up one breast and toyed with the nipple topping it, then slipped down into the deep valley to climb the other and repeat his oral assault. Glory threw her arms around his head and pulled him so close he thought he might suffocate. Slocum couldn't think of a better way of dying, his face surrounded by willing female flesh, his tongue flashing out, his lips kissing.

He ran his hands around her soapy back and then down to cup the twin mounds of her buttocks. He began squeezing and kneading, as if they were made of pliant dough. This brought forth an even louder sob of sheer pleasure from the woman's lips. Glory began undulating back and forth, shoving her breasts into his face and then denying him, but she made certain not to evade his firm grip on her hindquarters.

His finger sneaked between the meaty cheeks and

probed gently. This caused the brunette to cry out and twist away from him, turning completely in the tight confines of the tub. Most of the water had been slopped out, but what bothered Slocum was no longer having Glory's tasty breasts pressed against his face.

But for every loss there was a gain. She moved a bit more and leaned over the tall back of the galvanized tub, her rounded rump presented to him.

"Do it, John, now. I need you so! I'm burning up inside."

He rose to his knees and scooted closer. Reaching around her, he found those superb globes of breast flesh that had fascinated him so before. He ran his damp fingers over their sleek conical slopes and then trapped the nipples between thumbs and forefingers. Tightening his grip, he felt them respond. Blood pumped frantically into them, making them ever harder as he began twisting them about this way and that, stimulating her to shove her hips back into the curve of his groin.

His massive pillar parted the snowy half-moons of her buttocks and slid easily forward to find the fleshy doorway opening to her heated core. He repositioned himself a little more, then stroked forward, burying himself balls-deep within her. Glory gasped and sobbed, and a trembling passed through her.

"D-don't stop. Don't tease me like this!"

"You mean like this?" Slocum rotated his hips while remaining hidden fully beyond her pinkly scalloped nether lips. Every part of his manstalk rubbed against her inner tunnel and sensed the throbbing power locked within her tender body. He continued to manhandle her breasts, but he knew he couldn't maintain his position much longer. He slipped away slowly, drawing it out, arousing her—and himself—even more. When only the purpled tip of his iron shaft remained within her, he paused. The water lapped up against him and stimulated him to thrust forward right away. He had intended to toy with her a little more, to draw out her excitement and then speed up, but his own desires betrayed him.

Glory was an exciting, beautiful woman, and more willing than he had thought she might be after first meeting her. He had never intended things to end up like this with his friend's sister, but he had not forced her. Indeed, she had been the one who'd wantonly suggested that his bath become so much more than a simple cleaning.

He straightened, sending his spike racing into her. Glory gasped and then went crazy, thrashing about. He kept stroking over her breasts, kissing at her neck and ears as well as thrusting powerfully. The heat surrounding him began to take its toll. He sped up, creating even more friction along his flying length. The woman came fully alive, then cried out in carnal release. Slocum hung on and never slowed his pace. As her desires slackened, he accelerated his movement so his hips flew like a shuttlecock. He rammed ever deeper into her seething, moist interior, and then he felt her tensing again for yet another orgasm.

This time he was not able to restrain himself; his own passion had reached the breaking point. Deep within he felt the hot tides rising, then racing outward in a complete unchaining of any remaining control he might have. Glory gasped and Slocum spilled his seed. For a wonderful moment he was blind and deaf and taken away to another world, one filled only with stark pleasure. Then he sank forward, spent.

"Oh, John, that was so nice." Glory turned on the water again and pushed him down into the tub, gently washing him off.

"I never expected Caleb to have a sister so . . ." Words escaped him.

"So eager for what you have to offer?"

"Something like that," he said, realizing he didn't want to say what he had almost put into words.

"There," she said, her fingers lingering on him. "All clean."

She stood, and Slocum got to watch her gracefully step from the tub and bend to pick up the towel.

"Come along now," she said. "Let me dry you off." She smiled wickedly. "If you're a good boy, I'll let you dry me off."

"More fun getting you wet," Slocum said, climbing from the tub. He stretched and tested his muscles. A few bruises went deep to the bone, but the bath—and the amorous activity in it—had done wonders for getting him back into shape.

"Come on," Glory urged. "Help me towel off." She held out the fluffy towel. Slocum took it and began buffing her fine skin dry, giving a kiss or two as he worked. Then the brunette took the towel and returned the favor. She was on her knees in front of him, her mouth hovering near his quiescent organ, when Slocum heard a ruckus outside.

"What's going on?"

"Who cares?" asked Glory, but she reluctantly abandoned her oral explorations and grabbed her clothing. Slocum was already racing down the corridor to his room. He jumped into his other set of clothes, took his spare Colt Navy from his saddlebags and pulled on his boots, thankful they had dried out enough to wear. The shoes he had worn with the tuxedo had fallen to pieces as a result of the rough wear he had given them in Chinatown and after.

He reached the outer door about the time Glory did. Her clothing was in disarray and her wet hair was plastered to her head, but Slocum hardly noticed.

A shot echoed across the Presidio.

"That came from the headquarters building," Glory said.

"Stay here." Slocum tried to push her back inside to safety, but she had a mind of her own and ran ahead. Slocum quickly passed her and saw a dark figure slipping around the corner of the building.

"Stop!"

When the man didn't, Slocum fired into the air. This only lent speed to the fleeing man.

"Papa!" cried Glory. She ran to a man wearing an officer's jacket. He stood on the steps of the HQ building, a smoking cavalry pistol in his hand. "What happened? Are you all right?"

"I'm fine. But look!" Colonel Lawrence Newcombe pointed to the door behind him.

Slocum went cold inside when he saw a hatchet like the ones that had almost killed him in Chinatown stuck in the wood.

"Damned Chinee tried to kill me. I shot at him but missed. How the hell did he get onto the post without being seen? I'll court-martial the guard who let an assassin in to kill me!"

"Are you sure it was a Celestial?" Slocum asked. "Anybody can throw a hatchet."

"It was one of those sneaky yellow bastards. I know it! And who the hell are you?"

"Papa, this is John Slocum. He's a friend of Caleb's."

Lawrence Newcombe snorted in contempt and dismissed Slocum out of hand to bellow orders at the top of his lungs.

Slocum tucked his six-shooter into the waistband of his jeans and watched as the post commander assembled his company. From the way Private Carpenter stood at attention, shaking all over, Slocum knew who was responsible for the highbinder's getting into the Presidio to make the assassination attempt on the colonel.

He was glad he wasn't in the private's boots. But that meant nothing compared with finding the Celestial who had tried to kill Colonel Newcombe and learning the reason for such a bold attempt on his life. Slocum wasn't certain, but had a feeling it was all tied in with the beating he had gotten earlier. But how?

9

"I'll see you all in hell, I will!" raged Colonel Newcombe as he walked back and forth in front of the ragged ranks of half-dressed soldiers he had called out onto the parade grounds. Slocum stood back and watched Lawrence Newcombe chew out his troops, wondering how this was going to help. At Slocum's side stood Glory Newcombe, looking uneasy but not unduly upset over the way her father raged.

Slocum saw a bank of fog slowly moving up the hill from the direction of the Pacific Ocean and blanketing the Presidio. He marveled at the curious quality of the fog, both the way it deadened sounds and the way it teased with the opening and closing of tendrils moving about on idle wind currents. The harder he tried to peer into the fog, the more his head hurt. Slocum gave up trying, contenting himself with knowing that the fog cloaked his own presence equally with that of the so-called phantoms.

It was almost dawn, but enough darkness remained to give the buildings and distant trees an eerie, unnatural appearance. This, as much as anything else, spooked the soldiers. More than one looked nervously over his shoulder in the direction of the trees as he fingered his rifle. If the colonel wasn't careful, one of his troopers was likely to panic and start firing at anything that moved. Slocum decided that might be preferable to the colonel's wild, almost insane rage.

"Does he know?" Slocum asked.

"Papa? Does he know about us?"

Slocum looked at Glory and marveled at her one-track mind. Her focus was only on how her father might have found out about her peccadilloes; but then, she wasn't commander of the post—or its adjutant. Glory had no reason to worry about such things as troop morale, desertions or even untrained soldiers going crazy from fear and shooting anything that moved in and out of the thick fog.

"The ghosts and how they're affecting his troopers," Slocum said carefully. "Does he know about the desertions?"

"Oh, pish," Glory said. "That's all Caleb's wild notion. There might be some desertion, but there's plenty in all army detachments out West. The war's over, and nothing keeps the men in uniform except the promise of food and a roof over their heads. When something better comes along—and it is sure to in a city like San Francisco—they leave."

"So the high desertion rate has nothing to do with the phantoms?"

"You are too sensible to believe in ghosts, John," Glory said sternly. "Don't let Caleb convince you to believe something that's totally absurd."

"The tong killer trying to part your pa's hair with a hatchet isn't absurd."

"The Chinese don't cotton much to soldiers," Glory said. "The police in San Francisco are so utterly corrupt they allow anything to happen, as long as they've been paid off. Papa sends armed detachments to patrol the streets near the Presidio and naturally the Celestials hate him for it. They are so venal!" Glory sounded as if she was lecturing a small, willful, not-too-bright child. This rankled, but

Slocum pushed his emotions aside when he saw the calculating look on her beautiful face.

He had played enough poker to know the signs of a person's trying to get his goat so he would begin making mistakes. But why Glory wanted him angry was something he didn't understand.

Slocum watched the tendrils of fog drift across the parade grounds until he no longer saw the back three ranks of soldiers. But the incoming fog did nothing to dampen Colonel Newcombe's towering rage.

"Go out there and find the stinking yellow son of a bitch who tried to murder me. And Sergeant Thomassen, who were the soldiers on sentry duty when he snuck in?"

Thomassen stepped up and turned slightly, speaking rapidly to his superior. Slocum wondered what the sergeant was telling the colonel. From the expression on Private Carpenter's pasty face, the young man was sure he was going to be executed right there in the ranks for his dereliction.

Slocum stepped to the side, then sidled away from Glory. She took no notice that he was intent on going to find the hatchet man rather than on watching her father deride his soldiers for being incompetent. Slocum knew that if Colonel Newcombe had wanted the Celestial caught, he would have sent the entire company out to sweep through the Presidio and find where the would-be killer had gone.

Slocum reached the seaward side of the parade grounds. He had seen the hatchet man go in this direction and thought the path leading down to the ocean might be a good starting point. As before, he could not make out footprints along the trail meandering through the wooded area. Cautiously, Slocum started downhill toward the ocean. He heard the surf pounding against the shore long before he reached a spot where he could look out over a beach mostly obscured by fog.

This was the kind of weather favored by the Presidio's

ghosts. How the Celestial who had tried to kill the colonel fit in, Slocum wasn't sure. But there had to be some connection.

The rhythmic waves breaking against the rocky beach drowned out all but the most strident sounds, and the fog robbed Slocum of a clear view of the Pacific. He drew his six-shooter from where he had thrust it into his waistband and scrambled down to the thin ribbon of sand between the rocky stretch and where the waves endlessly lapped. Even in the dark, Slocum saw the tracks left in the sand just above the reach of the restless ocean. To his surprise, Slocum saw not one but three sets of footprints, all small and possibly made by slippered feet.

Slippers such as the Chinese wore instead of decent boots.

Slocum took after the Chinese at a jog, alert for any shadows moving ahead of him in the fog. Even exercising as much caution as possible, he came onto the trio unexpectedly. They crouched down on the beach, as if they warmed themselves over a campfire. But there was no fire, and the three all had wickedly sharp, long, thin-bladed knives in their hands.

"Hold it!" Slocum called, raising his six-gun. He wanted answers, not dead bodies. He was a good enough shot and had a decent enough range that he could kill all three before they had a chance to use their knives. "I want to talk."

The three men leaped to their feet but did not run. They faced him, a combination of bleak resignation and utter hatred in their eyes.

"I want to know what's going on. I won't shoot, but you've got to tell me why you're here and why you tried to kill Colonel Newcombe."

A shot muffled by the fog startled Slocum. He looked down at the six-shooter in his hand to make sure it had not accidentally discharged. Looking back to the Chinese, he saw one slumped over. The other two lit out running, heading south along the beach.

"Wait!"

Slocum's shout brought a volley of lead in his direction. One hot slug tore past his ear so close it sounded like a buzzing bee. Two more kicked up sand at his feet.

"Don't shoot. It's me, Slocum!" This produced a new round of shots, all coming his direction. Cursing, Slocum bent low, ducked and headed directly into the surf, where the fog was billowing and thick. He felt the clammy moisture touch his skin even as the ocean rose up to the tops of his boots. Slocum kept moving, then turned at a right angle and hurried through the fog and surf in the same direction taken by the fleeing Chinese.

He cut back toward drier territory and was met with a new fusillade. The soldiers had come down from the Presidio and were firing at anything that they saw moving in the fog. Slocum, unfortunately, had to keep running if he wanted to find out why the Chinese had ventured onto a military post to kill its commander.

Slocum stumbled over a body and fell headlong. He scrambled around, aiming his six-gun behind him. Slocum cursed when he saw a second highbinder dead on the beach; the soldiers' fire had downed the Chinaman. That left only the third Celestial to give him the information he wanted. Brushing off his hands and blowing as much sand from his Colt as he could, Slocum kept moving through the fog. Which by now had a faint glow from the rising sun.

The light had to filter its way over the hill and down to the ocean through the fog, but dawn was not to be denied. Though it'd be a while before the last of the fog burned off in the rays of a new day, Slocum found the going easier now that he could see the beach better.

Ahead almost a dozen yards he saw a dark figure dart away, heading toward the ocean.

Slocum brought his pistol up but did not shoot. It wasn't a Celestial he was looking at—it was a sailor.

He stared at the beach for a clue but failed to see the tracks left by the running Celestial. What he did see, though, was a section of beach that looked as if Colonel Newcombe had marched his entire battalion over it. Dozens of feet had churned up the sand. One broad, well-trod track led inland, up the hill into a spot in the Presidio near the cemetery. Slocum followed the dimly seen sailor to the surf and saw that a large boat had beached here and unloaded something.

Or some*one*. A lot of someones who had taken the trek up into the Presidio.

"Drop that hogleg or I'll drop you!" came the frightened command.

Slocum did as he was told, regretting it as he tossed his Colt to the sandy beach. It would take at least a half hour to strip, oil and reassemble the six-shooter. He turned, hands high, and faced six soldiers.

"Fire!"

Slocum went cold inside when he realized the order had been given to shoot him where he stood.

10

"Fire!"

Slocum tensed and started to twist about and dive into the shallow surf behind him to avoid what amounted to a firing squad.

"Halt! Do not fire!"

Slocum groaned as his ribs gave him a twinge from the way he had begun to turn, and then he relaxed. He lowered his hands when he saw Caleb Newcombe coming out of the fog, his pistol in his hand. From the way the officer glared, he might have shot the men with the rifles trained on Slocum if they had shown any inclination of carrying out the first order.

"Sir, that's not what the colonel told us," said Sergeant Thomassen. "You're interferin' with an order by the post commander."

"I am the post adjutant, Sergeant, and you will obey me. I am here and I order you to stand down. Stop pointing your rifles at Mr. Slocum. Now! Lower your rifles now!"

The four privates and the corporal in the squad hesitated, then obeyed. They looked at Sergeant Thomassen as if he might confirm that they had done the right thing.

"I'll report this to the colonel," Thomassen said angrily.

"Report and be damned," flared Caleb. "Right now you will bring your squad to attention. And you will join them until I give orders for you to return to your barracks."

"I can't do that, Captain. I was ordered to—"

"You are refusing a direct order by a superior officer? That's a court-martial offense, Sergeant."

Slocum saw the expression on Thomassen's face as he brought his men to attention, then reluctantly joined them. It showed how badly rusted the chain of command was at the Presidio that an enlisted man should ever have considered arguing his orders with the post adjutant.

Scooping up his sand-fouled six-shooter, Slocum tucked it into his waistband and moved out of the surf hungrily lapping up around his ankles; his boots had been soaked enough in ocean saltwater. As he moved he felt Sergeant Thomassen's eyes following him, like a hunter tracking his prey. Although he had done nothing, Slocum knew he had gained the noncom's undying enmity. Given the chance, Thomassen would have ordered his squad to gun down Slocum where he stood. Still, better to have the man hate him than kill him outright.

But where did the animosity grow from? Slocum had not planted any seed that would have brought the sergeant to the point of ignoring a command from his superior.

"Did you find the Celestials who tried to kill the colonel?" Slocum asked. He walked a few yards from where the squad stood rigidly at attention. Slocum could see how Thomassen's entire body shook, and it wasn't from the dank cold engendered by the fog.

"We searched the entire post," Caleb Newcombe said, shaking his head. "They turned into phantoms and vanished on us."

"Where were you when the highbinder tried to kill your pa?"

"I was returning from a patrol between the Presidio and Fort Point. There wasn't any fog, so I didn't expect any ghosts to show up tonight. Not then." Caleb looked around. The rising sun was rapidly burning away the fog bank that had cloaked the shoreline.

"Not ever," Slocum said forcefully. "See the sand yonder? A boat beached there and unloaded the ones you're taking to be ghosts."

"What about the highbinders?"

Slocum shook his head. "Don't rightly know about them yet. They're involved, but I can't read all the cards. Yet."

"What should I do with them?" Caleb Newcombe spoke more to himself than to Slocum as he stared at Thomassen's squad. "They'd have killed you, murdered you. I can't believe my father gave any such orders as the sergeant claimed."

Slocum remembered how agitated Lawrence Newcombe had been. He had left before he heard all the orders the post commander gave, but such a shoot-on-sight order might well have been among them. The colonel had been het up and not thinking straight. In truth, Slocum had seldom seen a commander lose his composure as fully as the colonel had. This alone caused Slocum to wonder about Colonel Newcombe. The man had had a distinguished career in battle. This latest brush with death shouldn't have made him so irrationally mad. Cold mad, maybe. But not so furious that he lost all sense of order and reason.

"Something's being smuggled into the Presidio," Slocum said. "The fog comes in and men troop across your parade grounds trying to scare the soldiers into looking the other way. Or running away."

"What?" demanded Caleb. "I'm at wit's end trying to figure this out. There's nothing on this green earth that would make such a scheme worthwhile. And why are the tong killers trying to drive a hatchet into my father's skull?"

"Any sign of missing arms?"

"What? No, I've been going over inventories for the IG's visit. All weapons are accounted for."

"Nothing's showing up on the post that shouldn't be there?"

"Nothing, except the phantoms," Caleb said, smiling ruefully. Slocum had to laugh. At least the captain wasn't chasing his own tail and griping about it. To the sergeant and his men, Caleb shouted, "Back to the post, double time. Move them out, Sergeant, move them out *now*!"

With ill grace, Thomassen got his men trotting up the steep slope toward the center of the Presidio. Caleb watched them disappear through the trees before he spoke.

"I'm not going to punish them. I ought to give Thomassen twenty lashes and reduce him to the ranks, but he might have been obeying orders, as he said."

Slocum remembered how the sergeant had spoken privately with Lawrence Newcombe. More was going on between sergeant and colonel than Caleb knew, and Slocum was not going to be the one to tell him.

"Did Thomassen have access to your office?"

"Could he have replaced the live ammo with blanks? Yes, he could have. So could almost anyone in the HQ building. I'm away from my office a great deal of the time—over at Fort Point, in the city wangling supplies, dealing with the San Francisco police over arrests of my men. John, I spend more time in the saddle now than I did in New Mexico."

They climbed the hill, following the path already taken by Thomassen and his squad. As they walked, Slocum thought hard. Something was being smuggled. If it wasn't ending up in the Presidio, that meant it was being taken into San Francisco. But why? Why carry contraband across a military post when a ship could dock along the Embarcadero and, for the price of a couple cases of whiskey as a bribe, smuggle about anything ashore?

And how did the Chinese hatchet men come into the picture?

By the time they reached the HQ building, everything looked normal, but Slocum felt the tension.

"Where's the colonel?" Slocum asked.

"In his office, I reckon," Caleb said. "There's nothing to report. We need to come up with some ideas that I can take to him to answer all the questions."

Slocum nodded, but his sharp eyes saw Sergeant Thomassen leaving the building by the side exit, the one nearest Colonel Newcombe's office. The sergeant had returned to the post, immediately reported to the commander and then made a point of avoiding the adjutant. Slocum was sure that Thomassen had observed them crossing the parade grounds and had gone out of his way trying not to be seen.

"Sit," Caleb said, pointing to the only chair in the office other than the one behind his desk. "We need to develop a plan of action."

"I want a tour of Fort Point," Slocum said. He turned slightly in the chair when he heard soft footsteps outside Caleb's office. Glory hurried along the corridor in the direction of her father's office. It struck Slocum that everyone reported directly to Colonel Newcombe, everyone but his own son.

"Why's that?"

"Whatever's going on has less to do with the Presidio than it does with smuggling contraband into San Francisco. I want to see if I can get any ideas what that contraband might be by asking the soldiers at Fort Point what they've seen or heard."

"I've asked them that already, John," Caleb said with a gusty sigh. "Nothing. They report nothing. And I believe them."

Slocum looked back down the corridor and saw Glory

coming from the colonel's office. Her report hadn't taken long. She left the building through the same door Thomassen had used, the one that didn't require them to go past Caleb's office.

"Let's go," Caleb said, giving in to the inevitable. "The quicker we get there, the quicker you'll see that I'm right."

The wind whipped across San Francisco Bay and almost took off Slocum's hat. He held it down as he faced the far side of the inlet, maybe a mile across.

"We can fire two miles," the artillery lieutenant with them said. "Accurately. We have the best gun battery along the Pacific coast."

"About the only one, I'd say," Slocum said, knowing the fort had been reinforced to repel any Confederate attempt to seize San Francisco and California during the war. To his right lay the island, swarming with the white seabirds—albatrosses, the lieutenant had told him. Alcatraz Island had been used as a military prison for some time and had a few prisoners now, notably Modoc Indians fresh off a rebellion in northern California.

"Nothing can get by us," the lieutenant boasted. "Nothing."

Slocum glanced at the proud young officer and almost believed him. The visibility from the battlements of Fort Point was exceptional. The guns were lined up and able to sink any unauthorized vessel trying to sneak into port, no matter what flag the ship flew.

"What about smugglers?" asked Caleb.

"We spot 'em pretty quick. They can't get into the harbor, usually."

"But they do get through. Often enough to make some trouble, don't they?" Slocum knew that any fort guarding the mouth of a harbor had to allow some smugglers to slip by, because no sentry system was perfect. This was what didn't set well with him. Why unload contraband on the far side of the Presidio and port it through a military post filled with armed soldiers when a little extra sailing allowed a lot less effort in selling whatever it was being smuggled?

"Opium, mostly," the lieutenant admitted. "The China Clippers come in from the Orient packed to the gunwales with the damned stuff. Sorry, sir," the lieutenant said. "Didn't mean to speak like that."

"It's all right, Lieutenant. I share your distaste for the drug," said Caleb. Slocum looked curiously at Caleb. The officer's words said one thing, but the tone hinted at something else.

"What kind of inspection is made once a ship has docked?" Slocum thought it might be possible that opium was being carried across Presidio grounds, but he wondered why, if it could be sneaked past the fort. Tons of it could be moved on a ship, compared with a few hundred pounds carried from Point Lobos on the far side of the peninsula.

"The city inspectors have been pretty harsh lately," the lieutenant said.

"Meaning?"

"It takes a lot more money to bribe them. About the only thing unusual along the Embarcadero are the tongs."

Slocum perked up when he heard this. "What do you mean?"

"There's a power struggle going on, the way we figure it," the lieutenant said. "The tongs want to control the waterfront, and the city officials are fighting them for it. Not a month back, the Celestials supposedly sank a ship that had come in from Hong Kong."

"What happened?" Slocum asked.

"I investigated that personally," Caleb said. "The best I could tell, the captain of the ship got into an argument with the head of the On Leong Tong—that's the most powerful of the so-called Six Companies—and got his ship sunk under him for the squabbling."

"Opium," the lieutenant said positively. "We don't know for certain but you can bet on it. The captain tried to short the tong, and they got even. Whenever anything like this happens, it's about opium."

Slocum nodded. This was probably true, but the lieutenant was admitting that a whale of a lot more got past Fort Point than the army could stop, or than the city inspectors even wanted to.

"We're ready for the inspector general's visit, sir," the lieutenant said. "We've got the whole fort looking spick-and-span."

"I wish the Presidio was in as good shape, Lieutenant," Caleb said. "Carry on."

"Sir!" The lieutenant stepped back, saluted smartly, then about-faced and marched away.

"He doesn't seem like the kind who'd lie to a superior officer, or to anyone his superior," Slocum said.

"Martin is a good officer," Caleb said. "Most at Fort Point are. The best are here, in fact."

Slocum continued to stare across the choppy bay. There was a question he needed answered, but he couldn't figure out what it was. He knew, however, that when he asked it and got the right answer, everything would fall into place.

"Let's get back to the Presidio," Slocum said. He wanted to get his horse and fetch his clothing from Madame Lysette's, then get his gun belt strapped back around his waist. Carrying his spare Colt thrust into his waistband was getting to be a bit annoying. He had no idea how Bill Hickok had carried a brace of pistols like this, much less been able to perform his lightning-fast draw.

As they stepped onto the road in front of Fort Point, Slocum caught movement out of the corner of his eye.

"Look out!" He dived, shoving Caleb to the ground as a bullet tore through the air above them. Slocum rolled to his side and got his six-shooter free, but saw only the sniper's back as he raced toward town. It was just as well he didn't try shooting the six-shooter so soon after it had been dropped on the beach and soaked in salty ocean water. He needed to clean and reload it before he could trust it to fire properly.

"I'll have him strung up if I find who shot at us like that," growled Caleb. The officer never asked Slocum if he knew who had fired.

Slocum thrust his six-gun back into his waistband, vowing to get his holster strapped back on before he went after the would-be killer. Claude Gorham's luck was running bad. His thugs had failed to remove Slocum the night before, and now he had missed what should have been an easy shot from ambush. Slocum wasn't going to give the mayor's assistant a third bite at the apple.

11

The brothel looked a little different from when Slocum had seen it the night before. Somehow the bright light of day turned it shoddy. Peeling yellow paint on the trim hinted at the decay within, and the heavily shuttered windows hinted at secrets held close—perhaps too close for comfort. Slocum ran his callused fingers over the butt of the six-gun shoved into his waistband as he considered how he ought to get his other weapon and clothing back from inside this now-foreboding fortress. Marching straight up to the front door was a possibility, but Slocum had little desire to see Madame Lysette again. And he certainly had no reason to talk with the opium-addicted Lily.

Simply walking into the house without bothering to knock might be a recipe for getting ventilated. The madam's bouncer might be laid up somewhere, but she might have other guards to protect her, her ladies of the evening and her property. Of all things, Slocum reckoned the woman would covet her property most, even to the detriment of her own well-being.

Slocum scouted the place and found a galvanized drain-pipe running up the back corner of the house that might hold his weight long enough to allow him to scramble into the nearby partially opened window. The best he could tell, that had been the room where Madame Lysette had given him the tuxedo and where he had left his belongings before going to the fancy ball. Again he touched the bare spot on his hip where the cross-draw holster usually rode. He felt naked without it in its place. Worse, he felt a tad helpless, in spite of his spare cleaned and reloaded Colt being close at hand in his waistband. It was a clumsier draw for him, no matter that many gunfighters had adopted just such a carrying place for their six-guns.

As he circled the brothel, Slocum got a prickly feeling at the back of his neck. Something wasn't right. Even though Madame Lysette's main business was mostly conducted at night, the way she had the place battened down like she expected a fierce storm to buffet the walls and windows gave Slocum pause. He might have been jumpy because of all that had happened at Fort Point and earlier, but he didn't think so. He wanted his other six-shooter and clothing, to tie up loose ends here. Then he could settle his score with Claude Gorham.

The uneasy feeling grew, but Slocum wasn't the kind to stay nervous long. Something other than just the look of the house ate at him, and he couldn't figure out what it might be.

Another long look at the brothel gave him no hint what was wrong. Slocum circled the building one more time, peered up and down Bush Street and saw only the usual morning traffic going on its way. Slocum rubbed his hands against his jeans, then climbed the drainpipe until he could stretch out a water-soaked boot and put his toe on the windowsill. For a moment he balanced precariously, aware of what a target he made from below. Looking over his shoulder, he saw no one drawing a bead on him, either behind him or in the street.

But something didn't feel right.

Slocum wasted no time using his toe to push up the window a bit farther, then bent perilously, fumbled until his fingers found purchase, gripped the sill and swung over. He tottered for a moment, got his balance, lifted the window the rest of the way and slid into the room with a loud thump. He paused just inside the window, listening hard, and heard voices elsewhere in the house, but nothing that sounded menacing. Slocum went to the wardrobe and opened the door. A sigh of relief slipped from his lips when he saw his trusty six-shooter and its holster still inside. He dropped the six-gun he carried onto the bed and strapped on his cross-draw holster. It settled on his hip and made him feel complete for the first time in over a day.

"You look better in a tuxedo," came Madame Lysette's voice from the doorway leading downstairs.

"I feel better dressed this way," Slocum said, glancing in the full-length mirror and seeing the strawberry blonde madam leaning indolently against the doorjamb.

"You do cut a dashing figure," she said. "And that gun might be more what I need that anything else."

"Even more than what you got from the mayor?"

Madame Lysette laughed ruefully. "That's business."

"Monkey business," Slocum said. "You want something from him or does he want something from you?"

"Both," Madame Lysette said. "You can imagine what he wants from me."

"Looks as if he was getting it, too."

Lysette turned no-nonsense at that.

"The mayor gets what you suggest, John, but he also gets a great deal of my money. It costs a fortune keeping this place running."

"Bribes, because prostitution is illegal," Slocum said.

"That doesn't stop the mayor, any of the other politicians or any man I ever saw." Madame Lysette looked even more dour. "Some women, too, seek my ladies."

Slocum shook his head. He wasn't involved in any of this and was sorry he had agreed to escort the madam the night before. All it had gotten him was a lump on the head and an abduction by hatchet men who mistook him for someone else.

"John, don't go." For the first time since he had met her, Madame Lysette sounded frightened. "I . . . I need your services. You're an honest man."

"Don't need *your* services," he said.

"I know you don't, not as long as Glory Newcombe is warming your bed and bath."

This startled Slocum. How did a whore working the fringes of the Barbary Coast, even one connected politically, know what had happened with Glory? And so soon.

"It's my business to know what's going on everywhere, John. I'll take care of the Walensky brothers and that no-account double-dealing Big Pete Ordway for you. That's only a few dollars."

"No," Slocum said. "I'll get them off my trail some other way. I won't hide behind a woman's skirts. More than that, I don't owe them anything, so paying them would be giving in to extortion."

"That's not the way it'd be. You'll be earning the money, and those tinhorn gamblers are a distraction to what is really important. I need you to protect me."

"From who? Why can't the mayor get rid of any of your problems? He's got to have some control over the police in this town."

"It's complicated," she said, frowning now. The longer Lysette talked, the more worried she became. Slocum might have thought it was only her way of getting him under her thumb, but he read people well enough to know something ate away at the madam. Something serious.

"Is this how Pierre got hurt?" Lysette jerked as if he had punched her. He had hit the target exactly.

"They're trying to put me out of business."

"Ask the mayor to help," Slocum said. "But don't ask his wife for help. She saw you go off with him at the dance."

"Here, John, here's a thousand dollars. That ought to get you free of your gambling debts."

"They're not my debts," Slocum said, his resolve hardening. "I don't owe the Walenskys a plugged nickel, and I'm not going to pay. It was my partner's debt, not mine. And I'm not going to cave in to a bunch of cheating gamblers."

"John, please. I need help. *Your* help." Madame Lysette thrust the wad of greenbacks toward him. "Pay them or not. I don't care. Let me hire you." She spun when a loud pounding sounded on the front door. Madame Lysette dropped the money, letting the bills flutter to the floor as she rushed to the head of the stairs and looked below. "They're here!"

Slocum scooped up the money, intending to give it back to the woman. He had no idea what trouble she had gotten herself into, but it was likely to be messy. Slocum had his own worries. Helping Caleb Newcombe was proving to be more difficult than he had anticipated, and he had a score to settle with not only the gamblers but Claude Gorham as well. Why the mayor's assistant had thought it a good idea to try to kill Slocum was a mystery, but the reason mattered less to Slocum than settling the score.

"Run, get out of here. Save yourself, John, then you can save me!"

The front door crashed inward, a burly San Francisco policeman tumbling into the foyer. Several more uniformed Specials rushed in after him, some with billy clubs swinging and others with their pistols drawn. Slocum looked past the madam and saw only death below. The policemen had blood in their eyes and wanted to kill someone—anyone.

He faded back into the room as Lysette started down the stairs, almost as if she walked up the steps to a gallows rather than down to speak with policemen in her own foyer.

"Clean out the whole damn place, men," ordered a man wearing the insignia of a captain. This told Slocum how far up the chain of command this raid went. Whomever

Madame Lysette had angered was capable of swinging immense political power.

"Be sure to root them out from the upstairs rooms, too," came a voice Slocum remembered from the night before. His hand clutched the butt of his six-shooter, wondering how hard it would be to put a bullet into Claude Gorham's worthless hide. Then he realized he would be pissing into the wind if he tried. A blue tide of policemen flooded up the stairs, rattling their nightsticks along the balusters as they came, creating a cacophony intended to strike fear in the hearts of any Cyprians in the house.

Slocum closed the door to the room and hastily shoved a chair under the knob. It wouldn't do more than slow the police, but it gave him time to gather his clothing from the wardrobe into a bundle and then get to the window. As he stepped out onto the sill, retracing the route he had taken to get into the brothel, he heard furious pounding on the door, accompanied by angry shouts. Grabbing the drainpipe, Slocum lowered himself fast and lit out.

Something told him to slow down and look back. Head out the window and looking around, Claude Gorham presented a pretty target if Slocum hadn't been out of range. Slocum considered taking the shot anyway, but the man vanished back into the room.

Slocum circled the block and came up Bush Street from St. Mary's Square in time to see the police shoving Lysette, Lily and two other partially clad women into a wagon, where they shackled them to eyebolts in the bed. Two men struggled to get their clothes on and stood to one side, talking confidentially with the police captain. Slocum saw money changing hands and knew who would end up in jail and who wouldn't.

He touched the thick roll of greenbacks Lysette had thrown in his direction before the police had broken down her front door. He had not asked for the thousand dollars, but he wasn't going to keep it, either. Slocum was torn between returning to the Presidio and settling matters with Caleb and seeing Lysette out of her jam.

The money decided him. He had to free her. Slocum returned to where he had tethered his horse, mounted and slowly followed the wagon and its cargo of soiled doves.

Slocum waited outside the city jail on Bryant Street until the sun began to dip behind the twin peaks at the western edge of town. He took notice of everyone who came and went, seeing the mayor enter, then leave within a few minutes just before dinnertime. But Slocum wanted to be certain where Claude Gorham was before entering. Gorham had been responsible for having Lysette arrested. Slocum figured he could kill two birds with one stone if he eliminated the mayor's assistant. Not only would he remove the source of Madame Lysette's trouble, he'd be getting rid of a man who had tried to bushwhack him. Twice.

As the sun dipped and twilight settled on the city, the soft hissing of street lamps filled the street in front of the jailhouse. Still Gorham had not come out. Slocum wondered if the man had left by some other doorway. The jail covered the better part of the block and extended back to Harrison Street. Finally tiring of the wait, Slocum patted the pocket holding the money Madame Lysette had tried to buy him with, then mounted the steps to the front door. He hesitated before going inside. Jails, no matter if he only visited or was incarcerated in them, always gave him the willies.

Seated just inside the door were two policemen, both armed with shotguns. One nodded off, but the other was alert enough for the pair. He came to his feet as Slocum moved farther into the large lobby of the jailhouse.

"Whatcha want?"

"I came to bail out a friend," Slocum said. "Where do I go to pay?"

A flare of greed lit the policeman's eyes, but it died fast

when a stout man with a walrus mustache came ambling over. He had shiny gold sergeant stripes on his sleeve, and the look of avarice in his eyes burned even brighter.

"Boyo, you postin' bond for a poor soul locked up in this fair hoosegow?"

Slocum nodded.

"Who might this poor soul that's run afoul of the law be, now?"

"She was arrested this afternoon." Slocum looked around and tried to seem guilty. "Don't want to talk about it out in the open. Wouldn't do having everyone know who was putting up the money."

"So who 'n hell are you?" the sergeant demanded. "Never seen the like of you before, boyo."

"I'm the agent for someone well connected," Slocum said. He drew out a small wad of the greenbacks and passed it to the officer. "He's looking for a bit of compassion, you might say, when it comes to Madame Lysette."

"Her?" The sergeant's expression changed. He licked his lips, then stroked over his thick mustache with his left hand as he fingered the money he held in his right. For a moment Slocum thought he was going to give it back. If the sergeant had rejected the bribe, it could only mean Lysette was in a world of trouble deeper than even money could plumb. The policeman's rapaciousness finally won out.

"Come on now, boyo. We got papers to sign."

Slocum followed across the large lobby into a warren of cells at the rear of the building. They stopped at a desk where a beefy policeman sat reading the *Alta California*. He barely glanced up when the sergeant presented himself in front of the desk.

"We got a special request, Zane," the sergeant said.

"Not takin' requests tonight," Zane said. "We're closed fer the night."

"A real *special* request," the sergeant said, leaning over and putting his hands on the paper, pinning it to the desk.

"This gentleman wants to spring the lady we arrested this morning."

"You know we cain't—" The officer's eyes widened when he looked up at the unyielding sergeant. "I gotcha, Sarge. A real special request." He peered around the bulk of the police sergeant and said, "You can go on back but you got to leave your hogleg out here. No guns allowed. Don't want them prisoners causin' us no trouble by flingin' lead all around."

"I don't want to *see* Madame Lysette," Slocum said. "I want to *free* her. How much is her bail?"

"You mean you and her, you ain't wantin' to—" The officer behind the desk looked irritated.

"I want to get her out of her cell." Slocum had intended to bail out Lily and the other two ladies of ill repute, but taking this one step at a time seemed the only way to proceed; let Lysette get her working girls out later. "I'm representing a rather influential party in this matter."

"He is," the sergeant said, winking broadly at the jailer, it seemed to Slocum.

"I got the papers right here," the man at the desk said, opening the bottom drawer. From where he stood Slocum saw that there were only empty whiskey bottles there. He went for his gun, but the sergeant was already in motion, swinging his billy club in a short, vicious arc that ended with a dull thud at Slocum's temple.

He had half drawn his six-shooter, but that was as far as he got before he slumped over the desk, unconscious.

12

"No deal, not 'less you throw in that fancy gun, too."

Slocum heard the distant voice and wondered who was speaking. The words were strangely accented and slurred. Most of all he wondered where the hell he was. His head felt like a rotted melon that had split open, his arms were cold and numb, and when he opened his eyes and finally focused them, he saw nothing but splintery wood. It took several seconds longer for the fog to lift from his brain enough for him to realize he was staring at the saltwater-soaked rough wooden planks of a dock.

When this fact hit home, dozens of other, lesser sounds and smells all fit into the larger picture. Seagulls squawking. The distant mournful sound of a bell on a harbor buoy clanging. The gentle slosh-slosh as water lapped against the shoring on the dock. The stench of rotting fish washed ashore. And Slocum knew that the man speaking was a sailor by his accent. He had heard plenty of the bragging old salts on the China–San Francisco route while he had been poking around in the deadfalls and dives of the Barbary Coast and knew how these men made extra money.

He had been careful then, because he had known he was in a den of thieves and cutthroats. Now, trying to get Ly-

sette out of jail, he had allowed himself to be shanghaied
by city policemen.

Slocum forced himself to listen and to try to understand what was being said. His life—his freedom—
depended on it.

What was the sailor saying about a gun?

Slocum stirred, moving as little as he could to keep
from warning the men who had slugged him that he was
awake. Even this tiny movement sent a lance of pain so intense into his head that his vision blurred for a moment. He
had been hit repeatedly and the cumulative effect was taking its toll on him. When he was able to see clearly again,
he saw scuffed shoes a few feet away, with a blue uniform
pants cuff just above. He didn't have to crane his neck
around to know this was the police sergeant who had
slugged him. And moving around nervously was the sailor,
his bare feet as hardened as any boot leather.

"I'm keepin' the six-shooter. It's got a nice balance, and
it shoots straighter than my service pistol."

Slocum fought to keep from jumping when he heard the
sharp report of his Colt, quickly followed by an aggrieved
cry from a seagull. The sergeant wasn't much of a shot if
he'd missed the bird at such close range.

"That there's one of them navy pistols. I rec'nize it. The
captain'd be real pleased to have it presented to him—as a
gift, mind you." The sailor made it sound as if the sergeant
was going to come out ahead in the transaction by staying
on the ship captain's good side.

"Go to hell," said the police sergeant. "Wait, you're already there, and you're fixin' to take this piece of garbage
with you. I'm keepin' the gun. I know it wouldn't be given
to no captain. Not this side of China. You'd keep it for
yourself!"

"Might be we don't want him. Just toss him into the bay
and let him wash up," said the sailor.

Slocum went cold inside when he heard that. Either

way, he was in a world of trouble. Drowning might be the more merciful fate ahead of him. More likely, they were only bargaining and would come to a compromise. If he didn't get free of his bonds fast he would be tossed, all trussed up, into the hold of a China Clipper and wouldn't be released until the ship was out of sight of land. Then he either worked as a sailor or was tossed overboard. He could swim good enough for splashing around in lakes and rivers but nobody made it back to dry land from the middle of the Pacific Ocean without a boat of some kind.

"Won't give you as much for 'im, then." The sailor wanted to barter and the sergeant wanted no part of it.

"I've heard tell Captain Johannsen is lookin' for crew. Whalin' ain't got the prestige to it that runnin' cargo back and forth from the Celestial Kingdom does, but what does this lowdown worm care 'bout prestige?"

"Look, Sarge, I got a quota to meet," the sailor said. "We're fixin' to sail with the mornin' tide. Got a decent cargo but not enough hands. I'll go fifty dollars for 'im. For 'im and the gun."

"A hunnerd dollars jist for him," the policeman insisted.

"Too much. You wanna bankrupt the good ship *Watersprite*?"

"Truth is I don't give a plugged nickel if you go straight to the bottom once you're outta San Francisco Bay—unless you give me the hunnerd dollars for this galoot. Then I might work up enough sympathy to shed a tear or two—or even wish for your speedy return."

"Sixty."

"Seventy-five and not one cent less."

"Done," said the sailor. "How you want the money? Same as always?"

"Ten tins."

"Ten! You robber! Eight!"

The men began arguing over how many tins of opium the sergeant would get for Slocum. He had heard enough to know he was in deep trouble unless he got free right away. Tensing and relaxing availed him nothing. The sailor had probably tied the knots holding him and had not allowed him any room to wiggle in.

Slocum flopped around a bit more, not caring now if the shanghaiers saw him. He grunted and strained until his muscles bulged with effort, but the ropes held securely.

"Lookit that. He's come back to the land of the livin'," said the policeman. Slocum saw that the sergeant had his gun belt with the Colt in it slung over his shoulder. The man's girth prevented him from belting it on.

Curses came to Slocum's lips, but he refused to utter them. He wasn't one for making threats. Both of these men would know his wrath—as they died.

"He'll make a good sailor. Be sure to take away his boots so he won't try to walk home!" The policeman laughed, then tucked the tins of opium into his voluminous uniform pockets and saluted mockingly. He strode off, whistling a sea chantey to further taunt Slocum.

"Come along, me hearty," the sailor said, looking around uneasily. "Won't do stayin' out where folks kin see."

Slocum grunted as the sailor easily picked him up and threw him over a bony shoulder. The sailor moved with the ease of a monkey as he went down a rope ladder to a platform under the dock. The darkness was almost absolute here, but Slocum caught a few glints of starlight off the waves coming in to break against the platform, where a skiff was tied. Already in the small boat lay two others, both securely tied. These men had gags in their mouths.

"The captain's gonna give me an extra ration of whiskey for this night's work. Three able-bodied seamen. Imagine that." The sailor dropped Slocum to the platform and went about his work, stripping back a tarp and loading boxes into the boat. Slocum considered tossing himself into the bay. He would drown, but that might be better than working as an impressed sailor for the next year of his life.

Even as the notion guttered like a candle in his mind, he snuffed it out. If he were dead, he could never get revenge.

Soft sounds came from the far side of the dark platform, and then a smell that he remembered well slipped between the fish odors to give him a surge of hope. He struggled to sit up to see what was going on, but a small hand pressed him down. Slocum took a deep breath and got a strong whiff of jasmine perfume.

"Don't move," came the woman's whisper.

Slocum craned his neck around, trying to get a good look at her. He was certain it was the same woman who had saved him from the hatchet men in the labyrinth below the streets of Chinatown, but Slocum had never seen her. She grabbed his head and forced him to look away, as if she wanted to remain anonymous.

Something in their brief scuffle gave her away. The sailor dropped the heavy canvas sack he was loading into the skiff and spun around, hand going to a wicked knife he had sheathed at his belt. As the shanghaier reached for his knife, Slocum felt the ropes on his wrists part from a quick slash. The rush of circulation into his hands was almost painful, but Slocum ignored it. He was free!

"Here," the woman said. Slocum got a glimpse of her. She was petite, dark-haired and Chinese. She thrust a jade knife into his hands, then slipped away silently.

"Damnation, I wanted you for the crew," the sailor said as he attacked. "Ain't gonna happen now." He tried to stab Slocum, but did not expect him to have a blade of his own.

Slocum moved fast, sidestepping the sailor's thrust. He brought up his hand with the jade knife in it, felt it slip into the man's rock-hard belly, then thrust upward at an angle and puncture his heart. The sailor uttered a strange liquid grunt, dropped his knife and collapsed without making another sound. Slocum pulled the now-bloody knife from the man's chest and looked down at him. He wiped the jade knife off on the sailor's filthy shirt, then retrieved the fallen steel knife and used it to free the two men in the bottom of the boat.

"If I were you, I'd get the hell out of here," Slocum said as the men sat up and rubbed their wrists.

"You done us a real big favor, mister," said one of the men. "We owe you."

"Take the knife," Slocum said, tossing the sailor's knife to the man. "If you come across any more shanghaiers, use that on their filthy throats."

"You don't have to ask twice. We got no love for those salty sea devils."

Slocum saw that the sack the sailor had been loading was nothing more than sugar. He used the jade knife to cut it open and pour it into the bay. Slocum wasn't sure what it might attract, but he hoped it would be something big and finny with an appetite for human flesh. He rolled the sailor's body to the edge of the platform, then kicked hard. With a soft splash, the man vanished from sight.

Stepping away, Slocum spun and went hunting for his benefactor. He owed her plenty, but she owed him more. She owed him an explanation as to why she had saved him twice, once from her own people and now from a shanghaier. Slocum got to the far edge of the platform under the dock and saw a knotted rope dangling from above. He scrambled up it and onto the dock, looking for any trace of the Chinese woman. There was only one way she could have gone, so he headed back toward solid land, but when he reached the foot of the dock he had no idea what direction she had taken.

The woman wasn't that far ahead of him, and she had been eager to leave, as if the sailor hadn't been her sole reason for being on the dock. He tilted his head to one side and listened to the diverse sounds of the Embarcadero. He fancied he could hear all the way to the other side of the Barbary Coast, but he knew that wasn't possible. The roar from the hundreds of saloons and deadfalls would have drowned out any possible sound.

He swung about slowly and tried to locate scuffling sounds to his left. Clutching the jade knife, he headed in that direction. The sounds grew louder until he saw two indistinct figures in front of a door leading into a warehouse. As one turned, Slocum saw faint light glint off a badge.

Policemen.

"Open up, you miserable Chinee whore!"

"Let us in and we won't do nuthin' to ya," promised the second policeman.

Slocum had started for them, intending to take them by surprise, when they were joined by a third man—one Slocum knew all too well. The sergeant with the bushy mustache strutted up. He still had Slocum's holster and six-gun slung over his shoulder.

"The yellow bitch is inside," the sergeant said. "We ain't gonna bust down this door—it's got a lockin' bar six inches thick on it. Around to the side there's a window that we can get through."

"We?" asked the first copper. "Since when did you put yourself out chasin' a sneak thief?"

"You two get in there. Come on around and open the door for me. Make it quick!" The sergeant kicked one and took a swipe with his billy club at the other. Slocum touched the tender spot on the side of his head where the sergeant had hit him. He was lucky the policeman hadn't stove in his head and killed him.

The two took off, and Slocum pressed himself against the brick wall of the warehouse as the sergeant took a quick look around before facing the door and rapping rhythmically on it with his nightstick.

"Come on, li'l lady. Open up. Open up or the big bad wolf's gonna huff and puff and blow you!" He laughed at this and began pounding harder. The sound echoed along the waterfront, but no one came to investigate. No one cared.

Slocum moved along in shadow until he was within a few feet of the sergeant. He judged distances, then lunged and grabbed his six-shooter from its holster. The policeman responded with surprising speed for a man of his bulk, spinning and bringing the billy club about in a vicious arc that barely missed Slocum's wrist.

"You sold me to a shanghaier," Slocum said, backpedaling fast, bringing up his six-shooter and cocking it. He pointed the muzzle squarely at the police sergeant. He thought this would freeze the cop in his tracks. He was wrong. The sergeant let out a deep-throated roar and charged, club whistling through the air in a furious figure-eight pattern.

Slocum fired, but the shot went wide. Then he was bowled over as the policeman crashed into him. Slocum gasped at the impact, tried to keep his balance and finally lost the battle, falling backward onto the ground, the man lashing out like an enraged bull. He tumbled onto Slocum and then lay still. For a moment, Slocum wasn't sure what had happened, then he remembered he had advanced on the copper with the jade knife in his right hand. When he grabbed for his Colt, he had shifted the green-stoned blade to his left hand.

He had missed with his six-gun, but the knife had stolen away the sergeant's life. The unknown woman had again saved his life, this time by the gift of her jade knife.

Heaving, Slocum got the policeman off him and struggled to his feet. He was still shaky from being tied up for so long after having his head almost bashed in, but he knew he had no time to recuperate. The woman who had hidden in the warehouse needed his help.

"Hey, Sarge, we caught her. She put up quite a fight. Real hellion, she is!"

Loud scraping sounds told Slocum the barred door was being opened from the inside. He barely had time to position himself as the heavy door creaked open.

"Move a muscle and you're both dead," Slocum said, shoving his six-gun into the policemen's faces. One froze, as Slocum had expected. The other moved with the same suicidal ferocity that had possessed the sergeant, and attacked.

Slocum fired point-blank into his chest. He dropped like a sack of flour and lay unmoving on the floor.

"Son of a bitch!" cried the other cop angrily, hanging onto the Chinese woman when she tried to jerk free of his grip. He swung her around and shoved her deeper into the warehouse. As Slocum was about to shoot him, the policeman ducked behind a stack of crates.

Slocum hesitated in going after the cop and the Chinese woman. A quick glance around showed only the two bodies on the ground; the ruckus hadn't attracted more of the crooked policemen to the warehouse. Slocum settled his nerves with a deep breath, then went after the police officer and his hostage.

Rather than following, Slocum cut immediately to the right and paralleled the warehouse wall while listening intently. He heard enough sounds of struggle to assure him he was on the right track. When a loud cry of pain echoed in the building, Slocum sprinted forward and swung around a tower of crates. The woman had bitten her kidnapper on the hand, provoking the outcry.

"Let her go," Slocum said, startling the policeman. The officer tried to pull the Chinese woman back in front as a shield, but Slocum had already drawn a bead on the man's head. He squeezed off the shot, catching the cop in the center of the forehead. The policeman dropped like a marionette with its strings cut.

For a moment, the Chinese woman stood stock-still, her ebony eyes fixed on Slocum. He moved to one side and approached, glancing from her to the dead policeman.

"He won't bother you anymore," Slocum said. She did not reply. Slocum wondered if she spoke English, then remembered her whispered commands to him. She simply wasn't up to talking with him. That suited Slocum just fine. "Thanks for cutting me free. Twice."

He turned to go, but the woman's quick, petite hand darted out and grabbed his sleeve.

"Wait," she said. He paused, not pulling away but not showing any sign of staying much longer, either. He had left dead policemen all over the place. When one of the crooked cops saw a friend down, he would blow on his shrill tin whistle and the place would be overflowing with blue-coated men with blood in their eyes.

"So?"

"You cannot go back out that way. They will kill you if you do."

"The police?" He saw a small shake of her head. "Your friends? The ones down in the tunnels under Chinatown?"

"Yes, the tongs. They fight to control the waterfront."

"To get opium?"

From the woman's expression, Slocum read that there was more than just opium involved. Distaste amounting to utter loathing washed over her pretty, even features, and for the first time Slocum got a good look at the woman who had pulled his bacon out of the fire twice. A round, moon-shaped face was framed by short-cut straight black hair. Intertwined through the hair were strands of what appeared to be miniature pearls. She wore a dark blue quilted coat that stopped just above her trim, slipper-clad feet. Unless Slocum was mistaken, the threads running through the fabric as decoration were real gold. Along with her use of a jade knife to cut him free, everything about her bespoke considerable wealth. On top of that Slocum could not deny the beguiling expression, the intelligent, bold gaze and the utter confidence she exuded.

And then there was the jasmine perfume that sent his

pulse racing. All in all, she was a trim, lovely package he was glad he had saved.

"What more is there?"

"We try to stop . . . contraband from coming to San Francisco," she said.

"Through the Presidio?" he guessed.

"No!"

At first Slocum thought she was emphatically denying what he had guessed, then he realized they were no longer alone. Movement observed from the corner of his eye sent him crashing into the Chinese woman, carrying her to safety as a hatchet tumbled through the air where they had stood. Slocum landed hard, twisted to protect her and then realized the hatchet would not have harmed her.

It was meant to kill him. He looked up to see four high-binders pointing six-guns at him. Behind them stood another row of the Chinese tong killers, all hefting their hatchets and trying to push past the four in front for their chance at him.

13

"No!"

The woman scrambled agilely atop Slocum, knocking his six-gun away. Then she did not move, her weight pressing down on him as she blocked the Chinese killers from filling him with lead. She spoke rapidly in the singsong language of the Celestials, but there was an edge to it Slocum had never heard before. She was giving orders and was mad as a wet hen that these men did not obey her instantly.

It took several more impassioned outbursts before they backed away, but the looks on their faces told Slocum he was living on borrowed time. He carefully thrust his six-shooter back into his holster. He might try shooting his way out, but would end up dead before he emptied the cylinder. It was better to let the woman try to dicker with them for his life, though what she might offer was beyond him.

The only bright spot in this predicament was that the Celestials were not likely to impress him into duty as a sailor.

"Outside," he said, hearing what none of the others had because of their argument over his fate. "Listen! Police whistles. They've found the policemen I killed."

More rapid-fire Chinese gushed from the woman's lips.

She turned fierce and pointed imperiously, as if such a tactic would work on hardened killers. To Slocum's surprise, it did. The hatchet men vanished tracelessly into the depths of the warehouse.

"Come, quick," she said, rolling to her knees and tugging frantically at Slocum's sleeve. "Policemen come after us. Quick-quick!"

Slocum heard the pounding of shoes against the ground outside, followed by the clatter of horses bringing even more reinforcements. The alert had gone out, and he was trapped in the warehouse.

"I can hold them off if you can get out," Slocum said.

The woman stopped and stared at him with her fathomless eyes. A small smile crept to her thin lips.

"You would sacrifice yourself to save me?"

"You risked your life twice for me. Three times, counting a few seconds ago. I don't reckon we're even yet."

"We will be," she said, tugging more insistently on his sleeve. "This way. Do not be afraid of the tunnels." The woman skipped lithely through the tumble of crates and came to a spot at the rear of the warehouse. Slocum heard the cops cursing as they found the last dead body he had left along the trail. He touched the butt of his six-shooter, ready to fight it out. This wasn't the spot he would have chosen to make a stand, but the woman had seemed to know where she was going. Instead she had led them to a dead end in the far corner of the building.

"Down."

Slocum started to ask what she meant, then saw a dark hole gaping under a crate half lifted by a wiry hatchet man already in the opening. Going headfirst into it, Slocum wiggled and flopped and fell a few feet, doubling over at the last instant and rolling away to come to a halt, sitting against the dirt tunnel wall. He looked up at the bright rectangle of light leading back into the warehouse in time to see the woman scampering down, using a ladder he had not seen. Then they were plunged into utter darkness as the crate dropped into place, sealing off the entrance.

"This way," the woman said. He felt a feathery caress across his cheek, then a firmer grip on his sleeve again. Slocum wondered if she could see in the dark. He had heard a lot of wild tales about Chinese, but never that they saw in complete darkness like cats.

As they moved along the tunnel, Slocum occasionally banging against the walls when the tunnel took unexpected turns, his eyes began to adapt, and he saw small points of light less than a foot above his head where holes had been drilled to provide air. Something overhead caused the light to shine down onto the dirt floor, providing tiny markers for those traveling in the subterranean ways.

When they came into a large room lit by several oil lamps, the brightness dazzled him, but Slocum squinted and got a good look around. Bunks lined three of the walls, giving quarters for more than a dozen men. Seated at a low table in the center of the room were four old men playing fan-tan. All four bowed slightly in Slocum's direction—or so he thought until he realized the woman stood beside him. She was the one on the receiving end of this deference.

"This way," she said, pulling at Slocum's sleeve and guiding him through the room to a small door he had missed in the far wall.

Slocum sucked in his breath. The outer room was Spartan and bare of any decoration. This one was opulent by any standard. Veils of delicately colored silks divided the room into segments, one with a pair of comfortable overstuffed chairs and the one farthest away holding a large bed with pillows scattered atop it.

"This is a mighty fine spread you've got here." Slocum said, looking around in admiration. The more he looked, the more he saw. Small brass lamps, elegant wood tables and low stools, a black-and-red lacquered cabinet—all the furniture and the rest of the contents showed that great wealth had been spent. For the woman? Slocum thought so, from the way she moved about the room with such familiarity. She was not visiting another's bedroom. This was hers, hidden under the streets of Chinatown.

"You are different from other Western devils," she said bluntly. The lovely, fragile-looking woman stood in front of him, her eyes locking on his. "My name is Mei Ling." She bowed slightly in his direction, her left fist hidden by her slender-fingered right hand.

"Thanks," Slocum said dryly. "It's always nice to know I'm a cut above other devils."

The sarcasm did not affect Mei Ling. She motioned for him to take a seat. Slocum sank down in the soft cushioned chair, grateful not to have to be watchful for someone trying to kill him. The only thing missing from the chair were arms for him to rest against.

"You try to stop the slave traders," she said pointedly.

Slocum nodded. He had pieced together the puzzle. Smugglers could get about anything to the Embarcadero if they paid the officials inspecting the cargo enough. He had seen how shanghaiing went on under their noses. The same with opium smuggling. No matter how much the soldiers at Fort Point bragged, smugglers would get past their guns.

The only thing he hadn't been able to figure out until he had heard that the Chinese tongs were trying to wrest control of the waterfront from city officials was what commodity had to be unloaded on the Pacific shoreline and brought overland through the Presidio.

Chinese slaves.

The tongs were strong enough to prevent unloading in the harbor, but were not able to completely stopper the flow of human flesh if it came in protected by soldiers.

"Do you know who's providing protection for the slavers on the army post?"

Mei Ling shook her head. "You try to stop them. We hear. You are a good man."

"A good devil," he corrected, grinning a little.

"A good devil," Mei Ling said, coming to him. She knelt on the floor in front of Slocum and turned her dark eyes up to him. "You have done me a great favor. You have saved me."

"You've saved my hide three times now. Might be more—I lost track," Slocum said. "You don't owe me anything. I owe you."

"We can repay each other," Mei Ling said. Her fingers stripped him of his gun belt while he sat in the chair, then worked on the brass buttons holding his fly shut. By the time she was digging around inside his jeans, Slocum was getting mighty uncomfortable. He got only a moment's relief when his erect organ popped out, standing tall and proud. Then the tensions mounted once more as the woman bent over and took him into her mouth. Her eager tongue swirled about the tender tip, causing Slocum to rise up off the chair and try to get even more of his fleshy flagpole into her mouth. But the moves he made were duplicated by Mei Ling so that she never took more than an inch between her lips.

She knew oral tricks that made Slocum even harder. He reached down and ran his fingers through her hair, tangling with the strands of pearls there. As he looked down he saw nothing but the reflection of rainbows off each and every pearl. Then Mei Ling looked at him, and he saw the glistening on her lips as they curled up in a wicked smile.

"You are very tasty," she said.

"For a foreign devil?"

"For anyone," Mei Ling said, licking her lips in anticipation of more. Slocum intended for her to get it. Now.

Slocum pulled her up and planted his lips against hers. For a few seconds they held this long, deep kiss. Then their tongues danced about, searching for sanctuary in one another's mouth like small children playing hide-and-seek.

When he broke off the kiss, he said, "You taste mighty

fine, too." But he didn't content himself with that. He wanted to know what lay beneath the elegant, if torn and dirty, quilted robe she wore. His fingers passed over her lightly rouged cheeks, past her shell-like ears and downward, pulling free fasteners as he went. The ornate twisted gold thread frogs holding shut the robe popped open one by one, revealing a slender body beneath.

Mei Ling pushed away from him and stepped back. Slowly turning, she shed the garment like a snake ridding itself of unwanted skin. The robe slid off her perfect shoulders, down her arms and exposed small, apple-sized breasts capped with coral nubs the size of the end of Slocum's thumb. The woman smiled a little more lasciviously and continued to lower the robe, to her trim waist, past hips and thighs and down to the floor, where she lithely stepped from the pile of unwanted clothing. Mei Ling turned in a full circle before him, clad only in her padded slippers. Then even these were cast aside.

Slocum couldn't take his eyes off her exotic beauty. The small breasts, the slender waist, the bottlebrush puff of jet black hair partly hidden between her thighs. She was perfectly proportioned, as if some figurine of a Chinese goddess had come to life.

"Do you want to watch only?" Mei Ling held her arms out from her sides, as if she modeled a fine new dress. She was clad only in her birthday suit, and it was about perfect as far as Slocum was concerned.

"No," Slocum said, getting to his feet. He shed his shirt in a flash and kicked off his boots. Mei Ling helped him work free of his tight jeans until he was as bare as she was. Then she came into his arms, melting like butter in the sun as she fit every curve on her luscious body to his workhardened one.

Their hands explored each other. Hers found old scars and new wounds; his glided over silky-smooth flesh the color of amber and found depressions and cavities both delicious and mysterious, making their exploration all the more exciting for them both. She stood considerably shorter than Slocum's six-foot frame, but this mattered little when he cupped her small buttocks and lifted her bodily from the floor. Mei Ling agilely wrapped her legs around his waist and settled down against him, wiggling and turning just enough to find the spike protruding upward from his groin.

They gasped in unison as Slocum slid easily into her velvet-lined tightness. Her ankles locked behind him as she pulled herself even closer, taking yet more of his manhood into her moist, clinging core.

Slocum began a slow dance, only his feet on the floor. Mei Ling swayed and moved and then pulled free with her hips just enough to allow herself a sliding, thrusting motion that made Slocum acutely aware of how close he was to exploding like some tenderfoot wrangler riding this fleshy trail for the first time.

He buried his face in the curve of her neck and shoulder, kissing passionately as he let her short hair swing about. The jasmine perfume Mei Ling favored was heady and stimulated Slocum even more, if that was possible. His hands continued to cup her firm buttocks until he realized she was firmly locked about him, her own hips moving and swaying and bouncing in experienced ways that he could never match with his more overt physical thrusts. Slocum kept one hand on her harvest-moon-like rump and let his other roam up and down her back, outlining each bone in her spine, running through her hair, moving onward, downward, around and across until both of them were gasping for breath.

Slocum fought to hold back the fiery tide that rose within him as the female sheath engulfing him began a slow contraction, squeezing and massaging, coaxing even more sensation from him.

Mei Ling panted and moaned and then fell backward,

supported only by Slocum's hand on her spine and by her tightly wrapped legs around his middle. This thrust him upward more powerfully into her tenaciously crushing interior. It took him a few heartbeats to realize that her passions were rising like the tide and were at the point of washing over her totally.

While she arched backward, his mouth moved from her neck and cheeks and lips downward, kissing the valley between her breasts. As his tongue slipped wetly over one nipple, the woman erupted in passion that Slocum felt instantly. He thought he had shoved himself into a fleshy vise. Her powerful inner muscles clamped on him fiercely as the tides of orgasm rose to hurricane fervor within her.

Tiny dots of perspiration beaded her forehead as she looked up at him. Her eyes were wild and animal-like. Slocum dived back into his erotic feast, taking one breast entirely into his mouth and gobbling hungrily. His tongue pushed one teat away and he dived onto the other, all the while spinning and dancing to music only he and Mei Ling were privy to.

Somehow they swung about through the curtains of silk, wrapped as tightly as if a spider had cocooned them. Slocum's legs tangled in the sleek silk and he fell heavily onto the bed at the far side of the room. The softness swallowed him as he turned and came out on top of the fragile-appearing woman. But there was nothing fragile in her demands as she unlocked her legs and brought her knees up to her chest. She reached down and stroked over Slocum's hardness, then insistently guided it back to the paradise where it had been lodged before they had tumbled onto the bed.

Slocum got up on his knees and moved forward, hardly able to hold back. Again he sank deeply into the woman's most intimate recess. This time he was controlling the speed, the depth, the duration of his trip. He sank balls-deep, then he pulled back and looked down at Mei Ling's passion-etched face. She held her knees up to give him the best possible carnal target. He was a superb marksman and did not disappoint either of them. Slocum began stroking faster and deeper, every stroke rocking the Chinese woman backward on the soft bed. He caught her on the rebound and sank even more fully into her wantonly offered earthy destination. As he raced all the way in to lock his groin to hers, Slocum arched his back and lifted slightly, as if trying to move her backward on the bed.

This was all the friction and tightness either could endure. Slocum loosed the fiery tide that had been dammed within him as Mei Ling once more cried out in the release of ultimate emotion.

Spent, Slocum sank down on the bed beside the woman and looked at her face. It had been contorted with pleasure moments earlier. Now it was peaceful, almost childlike. Or so he thought, until she opened those ebon eyes and fixed her gaze upon him.

"More slaves will be brought tonight."

Slocum hadn't expected this from her. Truth was, he wasn't sure what he had expected Mei Ling to say. He lay alongside, his body basking in the heat radiating from hers as he gathered his wits about him.

"Slavers never rest," she said.

"Who's behind it? Who organized this slave ring?"

Mei Ling sat up, partially hiding herself from him. She scooted across the bed and gathered one of the silk curtains that had been pulled down on their way to the bed. With a swirl, she swung it around her shoulders and only then faced him, her nakedness cunningly hidden once more from neck to foot.

"Such traffic in human flesh can be guarded only at the highest political level," she said.

"Just a politician?" Slocum knew that someone at the Presidio had to be in on this. Those were soldiers guarding the shackled lines of Chinese slaves dumped on the Pacific shore and marched through the army post. Not only were enlisted soldiers involved, their superiors were in the know. Slocum wanted to find out who they were and put a stop to it, for Caleb's sake as well as his own peace of mind. He had not wanted to get involved, but had. Getting shot at and almost shanghaied and involved with the lovely Mei Ling were all incidental to settling the score with Claude Gorham and stopping the infestation of slave-herding phantoms at the Presidio.

"We do not know."

"Gorham," Slocum said. The woman's eyes narrowed. She turned to cover her reaction, scooping up her quilted robe and donning it. She was completely dressed before she turned back to Slocum.

"You know more than I thought."

"Didn't know he was mixed up in the slave running, but I have a score to settle with him from earlier run-ins." He touched the spot on the side of his head where he had been slugged by the policeman. "He tried to gun me down, then sent me to be a crewman on the *Watersprite*."

"He is a busy man in San Francisco," Mei Ling said. "Perhaps much that is wrong will be right when he is no more."

Slocum climbed from the bed, wishing they could spend a bit more time in it. Instead he gave in to necessity and dressed, finally strapping on his gun belt and settling the familiar weight of the Colt on his left hip.

"What if Gorham is not there to receive the slaves to-night?" she asked.

"Doesn't matter. Him and me have other reasons to shoot it out. Only difference is, I'll be sure we're facing one another when the gunfire starts. I'm not a back shooter like he is."

Mei Ling nodded solemnly, as if understanding how truly treacherous Claude Gorham's attack had been. Slocum doubted Gorham had any idea how wide Slocum had cast his net. Madame Lysette, Caleb Newcombe, now Mei Ling and her people were all allied against the crooked politician. With odds like that against Gorham, no matter if he had corrupted the entire San Francisco Police Department, he didn't stand much of a chance.

Against John Slocum he had no chance at all.

"They only bring the slaves up from the beach landing site in the fog," Slocum said, thinking out loud. "That means they're afraid of being stopped. I know the Presidio's adjutant wants an end to this. Reckon most of the officers would, too, especially the commanding officer, since there's an inspection coming soon."

"We care nothing for any inspector of the military. We want our people freed. Life is difficult enough for us in San Francisco."

"You look to have a good enough life," Slocum said, indicating the silken hangings and remembering Mei Ling's sleek, smooth skin and hands. She did not work eighteen hours a day at a laundry or over a hot stove cooking pots of rice.

"I am emissary of the Emperor," she said.

"How's that?" Slocum saw she was stretching the truth a mite—or maybe unwilling to come out and tell the truth.

"I . . . I was the Qing Emperor's concubine. His favorite."

"The man's got good taste," Slocum said, but Mei Ling did not hear him. She was lost in her own memories.

"I fell into disfavor with the Empress, and she had the mandarins send me to this land of barbarians," Mei Ling said, staring hard at Slocum. He took no offense. He thought the Chinese were as strange in their ways as they obviously thought he was.

One thing he did not find strange was the way Mei Ling made love. From the way she had enjoyed their moment together, he doubted she considered this something to be disputed rather than shared. He might be an American and she a Chinese, but they were also a man and a woman. That transcended nationalities.

For a while.

"I report back to the chief eunuch of the court. And to the Six Companies. I forge alliances where I can."

"The Six Companies? You mean the tongs?"

Mei Ling nodded once. Then she went to a small teakwood chest and opened it, taking out a pair of jade knives. She tucked them away in her voluminous sleeves.

"The fog's coming in," Slocum guessed. He rested his hand on the ebony handle of his six-shooter and considered for a moment how alike the Colt and Mei Ling were. Ebony handle, ebony eyes, both packing immediate death if not handled properly—or even if they were handled properly. Both dangerous, both dependable.

"We should go," Mei Ling said. "If you will join me."

"Lead the way," Slocum said, talking to the woman's back. Mei Ling had already entered the labyrinth dug under the streets of Chinatown. He followed quickly, knowing men would die tonight.

14

Slocum had not realized how long he had been underground. Mei Ling stood in a darkened street, blending into shadow so that he hardly saw her outline until he stared straight at her.

"Where are we?" Slocum heard movement around them but saw nothing. From the odors, there were butcher shops nearby, and other shops with Chinese herbs and incenses, but he didn't know this section of town well enough not to need some guidance. He thought he heard a buoy ringing balefully out in the bay but couldn't tell what direction the sound came from. Small gray tendrils of fog slithered past dilapidated buildings and into the cobblestone street, only to become frightened and disappear like hesitant children. But every incursion was a little bolder, billowing and creeping and sneaking out to hide vision. Slocum knew soon the streets would be obscured completely by the moist clouds.

"Dupont Gai," Mei Ling said from her hiding place. "The middle of Chinatown. The man who directs the slave trade will be here to accept the new coolies."

Slocum moved toward the woman's voice and immediately felt the warmth of her body pressing intimately into

124

his. But for all the coziness there was a hardness to her now that he could not get past. She clutched a jade knife in her hand, ready to disembowel anyone who crossed her. She was tense, alert and ready to plunge that knife into a slave trader's vile heart.

Slocum hoped he got to Claude Gorham before the woman did. He wanted to settle the score personally.

"Do the tong leaders know who's running the slave ring?"

"Quiet," she said in a voice so low he hardly heard. Slocum fell silent, pressed back into the shadows and waited.

A carriage rattled along the street, as out of place here as a hat on a chicken. Two policemen sat on the front seat, one driving and the other clutching a sawed-off shotgun as if it were his lifeline and he might drown at any instant. In the back sat a man as cloaked in shadow as Slocum and Mei Ling. Hunched over a large suitcase, he looked neither left nor right but concentrated on the street ahead as if his vision could penetrate the increasingly thick fog.

"That's him," Slocum said. "That's Claude Gorham."

"Wait," cautioned Mei Ling. "He does not travel alone, this one. He is frightened always."

"He's got only two—" Slocum bit off the protest when he heard horses clopping along behind the carriage, hidden by the fog. Four more policemen astride horses trailed their boss.

"They grow careless. There are only seven tonight. Usually, we see a dozen or more."

"Could be a trap," Slocum said, but it didn't matter much to him. Claude Gorham had tried to kill him twice and then had set his crooked cops to shanghai him. Any one of those attacks had signed a death warrant for the mayor's assistant.

"It is," Mei Ling assured him. "For those who would enslave my people."

She tugged at his sleeve, then faded into the night. Slocum trailed her, loath to leave Gorham and his guards riding along the main street through the center of Chinatown. He found himself hard-pressed to keep up with her. As they walked quickly through the shantytown of Chinese sojourners, Slocum was aware that they picked up a small company of hatchet men. He worried that they might mistake him for one of Gorham's henchmen, then realized that they could have already killed him a dozen times over. If he stayed with Mei Ling, he was safe. The notion that Slocum couldn't survive on his own in this alien world locked within a more familiar city rankled, but he was forced to accept it.

They approached the Embarcadero, and sounds of boats rising and falling on the surging tide became more prominent.

"Here is the place where they sell my people," Mei Ling said, stopping Slocum and pointing to a burned-out building. Fire had gutted it recently, leaving the walls standing and little else. Somehow, they had arrived before Gorham's carriage and his guards.

"When are the new slaves supposed to be brought here?" Slocum asked.

Mei Ling never got a chance to answer. Gorham's carriage rattled around a corner and slowed. The policeman with the shotgun in the front seat spied one of the hatchet men—or had gotten spooked and opened fire. He blasted away with both barrels, ripping apart a tong warrior hiding in shadow down the street from the burned-out husk of a building. This inadvertently signaled for the attack to begin, premature as it was. The hatchet men rushed forward and were cut down by the two policemen, the driver with a pistol and the other firing his shotgun as fast as he could pull the triggers, then reload.

Slocum stepped out, lifted his six-gun and aimed carefully. His first shot tore a hole through the side of the carriage, flushing Claude Gorham like a pheasant from the brush. His second shot caught the cop firing the shotgun in the hand, forcing him to drop his weapon with a clatter. An instant later, he lay dead, a hatchet protruding from his chest. The sudden death of his partner caused the policeman who had been driving to bail out of the carriage, turn tail and run.

He'd gotten less than a dozen feet before an accurately thrown knife ended his life. By now the four policemen on horseback had arrived. They drew their pistols and charged, scattering the half dozen tong men swooping in on the two downed cops.

"Where's Gorham?" Slocum demanded of Mei Ling, but the woman was gone. He cursed. She had gone after Gorham without him even noticing. Slocum turned his back on the battle royal going on in the street outside the destroyed building. The hatchet men could handle the four armed police officers without his help.

Gorham's grunts and shrieks of protest drew Slocum like a fly to shit.

"I won't give it to you! Get away, you Chinese whore!" Gorham clung to the suitcase, turning away from Mei Ling as if this would cause her to cease her attack.

Slocum stepped over the stubs of fallen timbers and made his way toward them. The pair crashed together, fighting for the suitcase, then vanished into the ruins. He broke into a run when gunshots rang out. Mei Ling had brought a knife to a gunfight.

"Drop it!" Slocum tried to get a decent shot at Gorham. The man cowered behind a pile of red bricks, clutching a pistol in one hand and the large grip in the other. Slocum had no intention of taking Gorham alive; he only wanted to distract the man from his attack on Mei Ling. The tactic worked.

"You? How'd you get away?" Claude Gorham whipped his six-gun around and fired wildly. Slocum walked delib-

erately toward the frightened man, ignoring the hot lead flying around his head. When he got to a spot where he could
shoot, he did. Slocum's slug caught Gorham in the gut.

"Y-you shot me," Gorham gasped out. "Why didn't you
go away? You weren't wanted. Why didn't you die at Fort
Point?"

Slocum shot him again. This time Gorham dropped his
gun and simply sat down. He dragged the suitcase toward
him and clung to it as if it meant more than his very life.
Before Slocum could shoot a third time and end the back
shooter's miserable life, Gorham let out a tiny gasp of pain,
sagged to one side and sprawled in the soot and dirt.

Standing behind him, blood dripping from the jade
knife, Mei Ling simply stared at her victim. Then she
tossed away the befouled knife that had killed the mayor's
assistant.

"He deserved it," she said. "He has brought dozens of
my people to *Gum San* and kept them in chains to do terrible work."

"He deserved to die," Slocum said, regretting that he
hadn't been responsible. No man ambushed him the way
Claude Gorham had and lived to brag on it. Gorham had
dipped his oar into more waters than ambushing and
shanghaiing, though. Slocum figured Madame Lysette's
troubles were at an end, not to mention that he could now
walk along San Francisco's streets without looking over
his shoulder, waiting for a slug to steal away his life.

Then Slocum snorted. His life would never be that easy.
He still had the three gamblers on his heels and his dead
partner's debt to settle.

Mei Ling pried the suitcase free from Gorham's death
grip and opened it. The case overflowed with greenbacks.
She looked up at Slocum.

"This will buy the freedom of some of the men and
women he has brought here already."

Slocum had no interest in the money, no matter that

there might have been as much as ten thousand dollars in
the case. Another thought had come to him, a more troubling one.

"The fight started too soon. The new slaves—where are
they?"

"You are right. The soldiers who guard them will still be
bringing them here. We will wait for them and kill the soldiers." Mei Ling whistled shrilly and then called out in
Chinese to the unseen highbinders all around them. She
engaged in this one-sided talk for some time, then finally
ran out of commands.

"What do you do now, John Slocum?"

"I made a promise to a friend to stop the phantoms stir-
ring up everyone at the Presidio. Looks to be that the solution to your problem is the solution to his." Slocum got his
bearings, stepped away from Mei Ling with a nod in her
direction, then headed for the Presidio.

The gray fog closed in around Slocum, as if trying to
crush the life from him even as it stole away vision and
hearing. He took the time to reload his Colt Navy and be
sure it functioned well. He'd let Mei Ling and the others
from the tong wait for the shipment of human flesh to be
delivered to the destroyed building. Slocum had another
idea that had nothing to do with the slaves themselves.

He wanted to find out who protected them on their trek
across the Presidio on the way to enslavement.

Slocum wished he had his horse, but it was tethered
somewhere deeper in the city. As much as he hated the
idea, he had to consider the animal stolen by now. Having
left it outside the police station had almost ensured that it
was gone, taken by the crooked sergeant or one of his min-
ions. Slocum didn't mind walking, but the thick fog unexpectedly confused him and he found himself on the shore
of the bay. Cursing because he had gone perpendicular to
the direction that would carry him across the Presidio, he
followed the shoreline until he got to Fort Point, cut inland

and then backtracked, deciding that it was faster to keep walking along the sandy beach than to hike uphill and then back down.

Winded but undaunted in his quest to find the slavers before they moved their human wares into Chinatown through the Presidio, Slocum tromped along, eyes on the sandy beach for any sign that a boat had unloaded its cargo. In the distance, out to sea, Slocum heard loud shouts and thought he spotted a momentary flash of a lantern. He stopped and stared hard into the gray fog. For a moment it brightened, then the witch light faded and left him in the dark and cold.

A crunching sound farther down the beach brought him around, hand going to his pistol. He listened another few seconds and heard deliberate steps approaching. Slocum stared into the fog until he caught sight of a dark figure.

He started to draw, then thought better of it. He needed information about those responsible for the slave trade at the Presidio. Capturing a few of the men guarding the coolies as they marched them to their fate in Chinatown was the best way of proceeding. Slocum lengthened his stride and came up on the now-crouched figure. With a leap, he tackled the figure as it stirred.

And found himself with an armful of delightfully squirming woman.

"John! Whatever are you doing? This isn't the time or place!" Glory Newcombe stared up at him from where he had pinned her to the cold ground.

"What are you doing here?"

"I was looking for my father. I have a message for him, and the sentry said he had come this way."

"What's going on?" The roaring baritone question cut through the still night and brought Slocum around. Glory squirmed beneath him as he turned, throwing him off balance.

"Explain yourself, sir! You are forcing your unwanted

attentions onto my daughter! I ought to thrash you and—"
Colonel Lawrence Newcombe drew his saber and waved it
threateningly above his head, ready to bring it down on
Slocum.

Slocum's quick appraisal told him the officer would
miss by inches, but a second slash might land the heavy
weapon on an arm or hand. Slocum saw that if he drew and
fired now, he could put an end to any such threat. But Colonel Newcombe would be dead.

"Father, please! It's not like that. Not at all. Mr. Slocum
quite innocently collided with me, and we went tumbling
to the ground. He was merely helping me up."

Slocum had heard more convincing lies in his day. So
had the colonel.

"I challenge you to a duel, sir. An affair of honor."

"I thought the army discouraged that. You could get
court-martialed for dueling." Slocum wanted to keep the
colonel talking until his ire faded, but there seemed little
chance of that happening. If anything, Colonel Newcombe
was more furious now than when he had blundered across
Slocum straddling his daughter. His fury rose until Slocum
wondered what fed it. Any sane man would have listened to
an explanation without such wild-eyed rage.

"Father," Glory said sternly. "It is exactly as I said."

"It's a lovers' tryst," Newcombe raged on. "I won't have
any daughter of mine meeting with Southern trash."

Slocum rolled away and came to his feet. A rage to
match the colonel's filled him, then faded a mite when he
realized Newcombe was crazy as a loon. He squared his
stance as he faced the advancing officer.

"Come another step and I'll shoot you where you
stand," Slocum said.

"John, no! Wait! Both of you!" Glory climbed to her
feet and stumbled awkwardly into her father's path. The
two collided, but Newcombe caught her up in his arms and
swung her out of the way to keep after Slocum. Slocum

took a deep breath as he prepared to throw down on the officer. This would create incredible problems, but Slocum wasn't overly concerned. Not many folks in San Francisco thought well of him anyway at the moment.

"You were going to rape her, you barbarian. Sherman should have slaughtered the lot of you, instead of letting you live. Cowards! They were all too cowardly to do what had to be done—kill every last Rebel!"

"If you won't listen to reason, then listen to this." Slocum drew and fired in a smooth motion. The bullet kicked up sand an inch in front of Newcombe's boots. This caused the officer to stop dead in his tracks, sword half raised again. "I could have killed you, Colonel. I didn't because Caleb is my friend, and you've got this all wrong."

"Caleb," spat the colonel. "What's that pusillanimous pup have to do with this? You were going to rape my daughter!"

"I had her already," Slocum said, "but there wasn't any rape to it." Slocum thought of how eagerly Glory had joined him in the galvanized bathtub. There had not been any hint of rape; indeed, she had gone after him like a dog goes after a bone.

"You slept with my daughter?" This stopped Colonel Newcombe entirely rather than infuriating him further, adding to Slocum's idea that the commander of the Presidio wasn't in his right mind.

Colonel Newcombe lowered his sword and stared at her. Glory was turning red with anger now. Slocum didn't care if it was directed at him, her father or both of them. He wanted to stop the slavers from moving their human chattel, and this meaningless argument only slowed him.

"Father, it wasn't like that. Not exactly," Glory said. "Besides, it's none of your business what I do. This is so stupid!"

"I'm on the lookout for men dressed up as ghost soldiers leading Chinese slaves across your post," Slocum said.

"Are you going to marry him?"

The question struck both Slocum and Glory as incongruous.

"Father, let's go to your office so we can discuss this in a more civil fashion." She looked at Slocum, and he knew her pique was not diminishing. If anything, the woman was growing madder by the second.

"Very well. Accompany us, sir. We will thrash this matter out, I assure you. You will not have your way with my daughter and not do right by her!"

Slocum heard soft sounds back in the direction from which he had come, almost drowned out by the colonel's tirade. A boat had beached. Or perhaps it had already unloaded its cargo and was leaving.

"Hell and damnation," Slocum cried, shoving the colonel aside. Glory grabbed for him but he shook her off, too. Six-shooter firmly in his grip, he raced back along the rocky beach until he saw a new impression. A deep V had been cut into the wet sand where a longboat had come ashore. He wasn't sure but thought he saw traces of footprints going up the hill, through the center of the Presidio.

He knew the trail well enough by now to realize how easily ambushed he could be if he crashed along like a bull in a china shop. Better to cut around the hill and wait for the slavers and their charges as they crossed the grounds of the Presidio cemetery. Behind him came loud, maddened shouts from the colonel and only slightly less choleric cries from Glory Newcombe. He ignored them as he plunged into the fog, cut past the heavily wooded patch leading to the parade grounds and found the perimeter of the post cemetery. The fog was lighter here, fitfully blown by a faint breeze from the direction of San Francisco Bay. Slocum picked his spot and waited, taking time to reload. He wanted a full cylinder when he tangled with the men bringing the coolies to their new masters in town.

A chain clanking gave Slocum his first clue that he had

misjudged the time it took to get into the cemetery. He turned and peered downhill, toward the side of the graveyard closest to San Francisco, in time to see a faint, ghostly figure vanishing into the fog.

"Stop!" He aimed his six-gun and fired. The bullet careened off a marble tombstone and whined into the night. He had arrived too late to get in front of the string of men posing as phantoms and was close to letting them slip through his hands. Slocum pounded after them, only to flop to the ground when a rifle opened fire on him. It took several seconds for Slocum to realize the marksman shooting at him was not ahead but behind.

Rolling onto his back, he leveled his six-gun and then lifted the muzzle away from where Private Carpenter stood over him, taking a shaky aim.

"You ain't no haint," the private said, his voice cracking with strain. "I seen 'em, Mr. Slocum. Did you see 'em, too? I screwed up my courage and came after 'em, but you ain't no phantom."

"I'm not a ghost," Slocum said, getting to his feet. He looked from the obviously frightened sentry to the spot where the slavers had vanished. He had lost them again.

"I seen 'em," Private Carpenter said, as if sharing the most important news in the world. He lowered his rifle and mopped at his sweaty brow. "I went after 'em, but you was there. Reckon I mistook you for a phantom. Laugh's on me, ain't it, Mr. Slocum?"

"No, Private, the laugh's not on you." As much as he hated to do it, Slocum knew he had to abandon his hunt for the night.

He shoved his six-shooter back into its holster and accompanied the sentry back to the HQ building to deal with the colonel. He wasn't sure getting shot at in the fog wouldn't have been a better way to spend a few hours.

15

"I'm sorry that happened, John," said Caleb Newcombe. The adjutant looked more uncomfortable than he had any right to be—pale, drawn, hands shaking. Slocum told him so.

"It's everything comin' at me all at once, John," Caleb said. "I can't dodge it all, no matter how I try. And the way the colonel is always barking at me like a mean old dog . . ." Caleb mopped sweat from his pasty face, then stiffened a mite, as if he realized how he whined. He certainly was not taking criticism like a soldier and gentleman.

"You aren't responsible for your pa jumping to conclusions the way he did." Slocum did not say anything about the way the colonel had referred to Caleb in such a derogatory fashion while they'd been down on the beach. No officer, much less the son of a commander, ought to be chewed out like that in public. Slocum knew Caleb was inclined to let matters slide and to slough off insults from the time they'd ridden together in New Mexico, but this went farther than simple criticism. Slocum might not have called the colonel on his words, but he would never go along meekly the way Caleb had.

It was almost as if Caleb was afraid of something more important even than having his reputation and discipline over the soldiers in the Presidio compromised. What this might be Slocum couldn't say, but it had to be addressed or they might as well give up trying to stop the slavers from using the Presidio as their personal highway.

"I got you into this, John. I don't understand why my father didn't listen to Glory, though. He always listens to her. If she said nothing had happened, he should have believed her. I don't know what else I can say to convince him if he's not listening to her." Caleb looked beseechingly at Slocum, as if wanting his friend to assure him nothing had happened. Slocum wasn't beholden to Caleb, and what happened between him and Caleb's sister was nobody's business but their own. It wasn't Lawrence Newcombe's, and certainly it was not Caleb's.

"How're you coming with finding which soldiers are helping the slavers?" Slocum wanted to steer Caleb away from personal matters and concentrate on what was important.

"You sure Private Carpenter is on the up-and-up?" Caleb began to pace. Slocum couldn't help noticing that the captain's gait was unsteady—indeed, he even stumbled occasionally as he moved around the small office.

"The boy is innocent, if anyone is," Slocum said. He read people pretty well, and the young private believed in the phantoms so completely that his being part of the slave trafficking was entirely out of the question.

"I suppose I can confide a bit in him. Trust him to help. But not too much," Caleb said, talking more to himself than Slocum now. "He's only a private, after all."

"I'd concentrate on Sergeant Thomassen and see what he's up to," Slocum said. "If any of the noncoms has a part in this, he's the one."

"He's a good enough soldier," Caleb said, "though he has a distressing tendency to talk back. I never put up with his sass, but you might be right. He's the sort to get involved in something illegal, even Chinese slavery."

Slocum said nothing. He had heard Thomassen get away with wresting command from Caleb when they had been on patrol in the city. Although it was different now that the war was over, Slocum had seen irate commanders shoot a man where he stood for such insubordination. Even if Caleb didn't resort to such immediate, permanent measures, putting Thomassen on report, taking his stripes, fining him a month's pay, even putting him in the stocks at the corner of the parade grounds were all ways of disciplining him. That Caleb had done none of these things told Slocum of a rotted core in the discipline at the Presidio.

"What are you going to do now, John?"

Slocum yawned. It had been a long night. He had spent more than an hour with Glory and her father. They had begun by arguing and had ended after two in the morning with a wary truce. Slocum doubted the colonel would put up with anything more from him. That was fine, since Slocum figured he could clear up the problem of the phantoms fairly quickly. He bade Caleb good night and went to his bunk for some much-needed sleep.

But by the time reveille had sounded, Slocum was still groggy from lack of sleep. He had dreamed of Glory and Mei Ling and Madame Lysette all together, but it had not been as pleasant as it might have. He dressed and met Caleb on the parade grounds. The troops were assembling, forming ragged lines and looking like they all would desert, given the chance. Slocum saw that Caleb looked no better than he had when they had parted company hours earlier. If anything, he was even shakier.

"What're you going to do today, John? I have to muster the troops, see that they are drilled, get them ready for the inspector general's visit."

"I have to head out, if I still have a horse and gear," Slocum answered. He didn't want to go into details on how he had left his horse outside the San Francisco police station when he had tried to post bail for a madam. He doubted Caleb would have believed him anyway. But then, in Caleb's condition, Slocum wasn't sure the man could have understood anything. He was even paler and more drawn now than he had been before, though he did not stumble about as he had.

"You want a ride into town? We have a wagon going to Fort Point, then into the city for supplies."

"Thanks," Slocum said. "Anything that keeps me from having to hike any more miles is fine by me."

He rode in the back of the flatbed wagon to a store less than a mile from Madame Lysette's brothel. Slocum checked his six-shooter before setting off for the house on Bush Street. For once he didn't spend a great deal of time backtracking and looking over his shoulder. Claude Gorham's death had removed some of the uncertainty from walking about town for him, even if he'd still have to deal with a trio of rough-and-tumble gamblers eventually. But the Walensky brothers and their partner, Big Pete Ordway, could wait a while longer.

To his surprise, Madame Lysette sat on her front porch genteelly sipping at tea as he came up the front walk. When she saw him, she put down her china teacup and rushed to him.

"John, you are a miracle worker!" she cried. "I hoped that you could get me out of that awful place, and you did!"

"I didn't kill Gorham," he said. This seemed to shock Madame Lysette. "You didn't know?" he asked. For once he had a tidbit of gossip that hadn't been filtered through the madam's web of informers.

"No," she said. "I am embarrassed, Mr. Slocum. I take pride in knowing things like this. What happened? No, don't tell me. I'll find out on my own."

"The highbinders took him out of the game," Slocum said, not stretching the truth too much and not caring about the woman's pride in unearthing such information herself. Considering that Gorham was killed in Chinatown, the story might get confused, and Slocum wanted it set straight from the start. "He was mixed up in slave trading, and the Six Companies put a stop to it—and him."

"I knew Gorham was a low-down insect," Madame Lysette said, taking Slocum's arm and steering him to her front porch, where he sat down opposite her. She poured him a cup of tea. Slocum was almost afraid to take the cup for fear of breaking it. The fine bone china was mighty fragile. After a sip of the tea, he was sorry he had bothered. He preferred coffee boiled over a campfire. This swill was more like dirty water than anything fit to drink, but he politely finished it in a gulp to be done with it. Lysette refilled his cup before he could protest.

"He was so crooked he made a dog's hind leg look like an arrow," Madame Lysette went on. "He and the mayor's wife were having an affair, not so much because he was a lecher but because it kept him close to the mayor and the power he wields. When Gorham saw how close I was getting to the mayor and how that old dear would never do a thing to inconvenience me, that's when he tried to muscle in."

"How did you get out of jail?" Slocum touched the lump in his shirt pocket, where most all of the thousand dollars she had given him still rode high, wide and fancy free.

"I thought you had arranged bail. I didn't stop to ask questions when the jailer opened the cell door."

Slocum considered the timing. Gorham's death might have endangered a lot of shady schemes in San Francisco. If the police officer in charge of the city jail knew of Madame Lysette's connection with the mayor—and such news had to be readily available—he might have released her. Without Gorham's protection, any such incarceration could turn in a flash against the men responsible.

"Actually, I can't imagine why Gorham wanted me shut down like he so obviously did. I would gladly have paid him off. Double! Bribery is a way of doing business in this town. What was one more hand dipping into the till?"

"I think I know," Slocum said, putting more of the pieces of the crazy quilt together.

"Why? Again, Mr. Slocum, it is distressing to me that I don't know the answers to questions that should be my stock and trade."

"Your stock and trade is female flesh," Slocum said.

"That is a bit blunt, sir," Madame Lysette said with mock indignation. "But true." She smiled and had started to pour even more tea into his cup when he put his hand over the brim to prevent it.

"Do you mind if I send for a friend to confirm my guess about Claude Gorham and what he was up to? Having her come here might not be a good idea, but it would be a worse one for you to go to her."

"How intriguing, Mr. Slocum. But then you are an intriguing man." The blonde batted her long, dark eyelashes in his direction, but Slocum was no more interested in her wiles than he was in her watery tea. Seeing she had no power over him, she snapped her fingers. A young boy of seven or eight appeared.

"He your message boy?" Slocum asked.

"Give him your message and tell him to whom it should be delivered. It doesn't matter where in San Francisco it has to go. Jethro moves as easily in high society as he does in the Barbary Coast."

"Do you know Chinatown?" asked Slocum. "Take this to Mei Ling. Ask for her anywhere along Dupont Gai."

"My, my, you do get around," Madame Lysette said. "Always a surprise in store. That's what I like about you. One of the many things," she said, batting her eyelashes once more in an attempt to be coy. Slocum hardly noticed. He was too busy considering what had to be done—and who to do it to.

The tension was enough to make anyone jumpy. Slocum was seated across the table from Madame Lysette, with

Mei Ling between them. The Chinese woman sat rigidly, hands folded in her lap. She occasionally sampled the tea, but otherwise made no effort to be polite.

"Enough of this," Madame Lysette finally said, after they had danced around a few minutes and then shared a silence stretched all the way across the bay to Tiburón. "Why's she here, Mr. Slocum?"

"'Less I miss my guess, you two had a mutual enemy."

The women exchanged glances, Mei Ling quickly averting her eyes again. Then they said in unison, "Claude Gorham."

Madame Lysette laughed at the incongruity and said, "Mr. Gorham certainly got around, causing trouble at City Hall, here, in the Barbary Coast, and now, we find, in Chinatown. What was that knave up to?"

"He was bringing in women slaves to sell to whorehouses," Slocum said. This brought Mei Ling's dark eyes up to fix on him like twin beacons. "Don't know if he had already set up the brothels or if he intended to do it later, but it makes sense that he wanted Chinese women for whores."

"Why?" Mei Ling spoke precisely, brooking no argument. She would have an answer that made sense to her.

"Because he tried to put Madame Lysette out of business. She paid him off, but that wasn't good enough. He still had her jailed."

"I'm out of business so he can run his ladies in Chinatown? Hmm," Lysette said, sipping at her tea as she thought on it. "There ought to be enough, shall we say, vice to go around."

"Not for a man as greedy as Claude Gorham," Slocum said. "He wanted a monopoly on the trade in human flesh, both coming into San Francisco and after it got here."

"I have heard rumors," Mei Ling said softly. "No Chinese would run such an establishment."

"Really, dearie?" Madame Lysette laughed. "Ah Toy runs a high-class joint south of town."

"She does not use slaves," Mei Ling said, her cheeks flushing slightly as she fought to hold anger in check.

"You're so self-righteous," Madame Lysette said. "You people—"

"Ladies, we have a great deal to do," Slocum said, trying to be as diplomatic as possible. "It's in all our interests to stop the slaves."

"Why is it in yours, Mr. Slocum?" asked Madame Lysette.

"A friend in the Presidio wants it stopped and can't get a handle on it," he said, bending the truth a mite. Although Caleb Newcombe might know what was going on, he was less interested in Chinese slave traders than he was in preventing more desertions from his battalion. The local police, not the military, were responsible for law enforcement in San Francisco, even if they were crooked scoundrels.

"So, a man of honor to the end. Yes, I was right about you, Mr. Slocum," the madam said. "A true Southern gentleman."

"What can I do to help?" demanded Mei Ling.

"Well, dearie, you might start with that cathouse behind the Hangah Pagoda two blocks west of Portsmouth Square. If dear Claude wanted to dip his, hmm, oar into the waters of the world's oldest profession, that would be the den of iniquity he would choose."

"You know this place?" Slocum asked Mei Ling. He saw that she did. He realized she probably knew of many brothels in and around Chinatown, a fact that would fly in the face of her assertion that no Chinese woman would ever engage in prostitution. "Let's go."

As they went down the steps, Lysette reached out and took Slocum by the arm. In a low voice, but one loud enough for Mei Ling to hear, the strawberry blonde said, "Wait a moment. I almost forgot: I have your horse and gear around back. They let me take them when I left that horrid jail."

"Much obliged," Slocum said. He had thought both horse and belongings were long gone.

"When you're done, come back and I can thank you in an even better way, Mr. Slocum." Again Madame Lysette batted her eyelashes and gave him her winning smile.

He touched the brim of his hat politely so he wouldn't have to say anything and joined Mei Ling, who had walked on slowly and waited at the curb. As he got to her side he heard her mutter, "Even the tea was old and tasteless."

Slocum fetched his horse from behind the brothel and he and Mei Ling rode to the corner of Chinese and Duncombe Streets, Slocum glad to be back in the saddle again. It didn't hurt any having Mei Ling riding behind him, her slender arms circling his waist, either.

"There is the place," the woman said with some distaste. "How does she know such things?"

"It's her business to know," Slocum said. "She keeps a sharp eye on competition."

Slocum looked around and saw they had picked up a considerable entourage of Chinese men, all trying to remain in doorways and around corners but obviously watching him and Mei Ling.

"Are those your men?" he asked.

"Some are. Enough to protect me. I am, after all, the Emperor's concubine." She made this sound somewhat more exalted than being Empress, although Slocum remembered that it had been the Empress who had shanghaied Mei Ling to San Francisco. That put into perspective where the real power lay in China.

"What will you do with the women when they're freed?" Slocum asked.

Mei Ling tensed and put some distance between herself and the portion of Slocum against which she had pressed closely during the ride. For a moment Slocum thought she was not going to answer, but she finally did.

"They will find other jobs. There are many establishments in Chinatown where they can work honorably."

Slocum wondered how it was honorable for Mei Ling to be the Emperor's whore, while working as a prostitute in this rather austere house wasn't. The action was the same, even if the pay and privileges weren't. But he quickly forgot the question, because he was opposed to keeping women as sex slaves no matter who the keeper was. That Claude Gorham had had a hand in this whorehouse would make it doubly pleasant to put it out of business.

"How do we go about it?" Mei Ling asked.

"I go in like I'm looking for some feminine companionship, get the lay of the land, then signal to you so your men can come in and remove the women."

"The 'lay of the land'?" Mei Ling laughed. "You will not find such a thing in *that* place."

"Where will I?" Slocum asked jokingly.

"Afterward, I shall show you."

Mei Ling slid from behind him and hurried off to speak with a smallish Chinese man with bent shoulders and a heavily scarred face who came from inside a laundry. They spoke rapidly, then he shuffled off, his feet moving almost too fast to be seen. Slocum saw how the man hurried down the street, apparently saying nothing, but one after another of the highbinders would move in the direction of the cathouse after the laundryman passed them.

It was time for him to do what he could. Slocum doubted his horse would be stolen while he was working so closely with Mei Ling, so he swung the reins around a hitching post on the street, then went up the walk to the front door and knocked. He was getting ready to knock again when the door opened on well-oiled hinges. Slocum saw that the door was sturdier than it appeared from the outside and might withstand considerable kicking and banging. A quick glance past the hulking man who answered showed the place was closer to a fortress than a parlor house such as Madame Lysette ran.

This whorehouse's clientele was more likely to be rowdy and need escorting out.

"Whatya want?" The man was easily Slocum's six feet but weighed fifty pounds more. From the tattoos on the backs of his hands and forearms, he had worked as a sailor. When he flexed his muscles in an obvious attempt to intimidate Slocum, the seams of his cambric shirt threatened to pop.

"Heard tell from a friend that this was a good place to find some pretty Chinee girls."

"Who's yer friend?"

"A gent named Gorham. Claude Gorham." Slocum knew he had hit the target by the man's reaction. The bouncer started to slam the door, but Slocum was already lunging forward to get his shoulder into the heavy wood panels. It felt as if he slammed into a brick wall, then his momentum carried him on into the room beyond. The bouncer staggered back, arms flailing about to keep his balance.

"It's the cops!" the giant shouted as he recovered. With a deep growl he lumbered toward Slocum, fists clenched tightly and tendons standing out like wire rope on his forearms. The nasty look on his face told the story, even if Slocum hadn't been smart enough to otherwise figure out this was one mean galoot intent on separating his arms and legs from his torso.

Slocum somersaulted past the man's groping arms and came to his feet, six-shooter out and ready. The bouncer took no notice of the gun as he lunged, missing Slocum by inches. He spun around like an animal and prepared for another attack.

"Gonna kill you. Yer no friend of Mr. Gorham."

Slocum glanced to the rear of the room, and through a

door leading into a corridor saw two more men hustling partially clad Chinese women out of their rooms. He turned back to the bouncer and aimed the six-gun directly at the man's face.

"Do I have to shoot you?" Slocum was only partly bluffing. He fired when the bouncer charged, head down like an angry bull. The bullet tore a bloody track across the man's heavily muscled shoulder—and then Slocum was carried backward in an embrace that felt like steel bands were tightening around his arms. Although his arms were pinned at his sides, Slocum was able to fire again. This bullet caught the bouncer in the thigh. A grunt was all the reaction Slocum got from the man.

"Gonna kill you, you dirty copper!"

Slocum tried to fire again, but his arms were going numb. He kicked and fought as the life was about to be squeezed from his body. Then, as suddenly as the pressure had been applied, it was released. Slocum fell back, gasping for air.

Standing behind the dead bouncer was a hatchet man holding his bloody weapon.

"In the back. They're trying to get away," Slocum gasped.

He got to his feet and went out the way he had come in. Mei Ling's men swarmed into the house, shouting in Chinese. Slocum didn't much care what they were calling, only that it was enough to spook the white men he had spotted down the hall, who undoubtedly were the women's jailers.

Meaty thuds echoed from the house as the fight got more brutal. Slocum vaulted a low fence and ran to the north side of the house in time to grab hold of a man trying to wiggle up through a cellar window and escape. Slocum swung the man around and pinned him to the ground, only to hear someone else coming out of the cellar. Slocum half turned and was struck on the head by something hard and heavy.

He fell to the side and lay stunned. His vision cleared enough to see the man he had tried to catch fall with a hatchet in his back. But Slocum wondered if he was entirely in his head as he saw the person who had slugged him getting away down the street.

There was no mistaking the sleek, slim, brunette Glory Newcombe.

16

"How many?" Slocum asked, seeing the tight knot of mostly naked young Chinese women huddled together inside the doorway. He couldn't help thinking of the women at Madame Lysette's brothel. Lily might have been an opium addict, but she had some value to the madam, who was willing to try to break her dependence on the drug. None of these women were in the least well cared for. Slocum saw bruises, cuts, filthy, matted hair and more vermin crawling around on their bodies than he'd likely find on week-old corpses in a battlefield.

Rescuing them had been a decent thing to do, no matter that it was getting back at Claude Gorham.

"You saw?" asked Mei Ling. He didn't have to get her to explain what she meant.

"Did you find anything linking her to this place?"

"Only boxes of money," said Mei Ling. She held out a bucket filled with coins, mostly dimes and two-bit pieces. This was probably the going rate for a tumble with the slave girls.

"No documents?"

Mei Ling let out a chirp like a bird, then shook her head. "Such ones never implicate themselves. Documents would not be necessary to assert her power in such a place."

Slocum found himself unconsciously slipping his six-gun halfway from his holster, then dropping it back, repeating the action over and over. Telling Caleb that his sister was involved in the slave ring—and might be the principal—rankled. Caleb couldn't have had a clue Glory was mixed up in this when he'd asked Slocum to investigate. Slocum felt a surge of distaste for Glory when he realized she had joined him in his bath only to cloud his judgment, to find out what he knew, to keep an eye on someone who might upset her profitable applecart.

He was glad he had killed Claude Gorham; he wasn't so sure what the appropriate punishment for Glory Newcombe ought to be. In some ways he felt it should be worse, but he wasn't certain he was up to being the one to deliver such retribution on her pretty head.

"Fourteen," Mei Ling said. "We have found fourteen damaged flowers from the Celestial Kingdom under this roof. Thank you for your aid in freeing them, John." Mei Ling bowed deeper than she ever had before. Slocum distantly realized this was a measure of her respect for him, but he dismissed it with the wave of a hand.

"Work's just started," he said. "Take care of those girls, then ask Madame Lysette for more addresses. I'm sure this isn't the only place Gorham was supplying."

"I will send such a request," Mei Ling said, obviously not wanting anything more to do with Madame Lysette. She turned her face upward to Slocum's and grinned. "I must allow others to share the gracious madam's indescribable tea."

Slocum knew he had put off tracking Glory and resolving her part in the mess long enough, but he found it hard to part company with Mei Ling. The Celestial went about ordering the hatchet men as if they were small children, and they obeyed. Slocum marveled at this, since he had seen how ruthless these highbinders were when it came to killing. Mei Ling might well have been a powerful concubine in the Emperor's entourage, and Slocum pitied the Empress when Mei Ling finally returned to the Flowery Kingdom.

He looked around for any sign that the slavers might have spies posted, but the only faces he saw were Chinese. It wouldn't take long for word to spread to other brothels where Chinese women were being held prisoner. He wondered if this single raid might start the row of dominoes falling over and lead to the release of all the slaves.

He doubted it, the way things were in this city. Slocum mounted, rode for the Presidio and vowed to get the hell out of San Francisco as quickly as he could. The tall mountains shrouded in decent fog, with fragrant pine trees poking up everywhere and lakes, meadows and sheer *quiet,* all drew him more than ever, especially since the clatter of hooves' hooves on the pavement, wagons and other commerce created such a constant head-splitting din.

The only smell of this town he would miss would be Mei Ling's jasmine perfume.

He set off riding slowly toward the Presidio, wondering if he had actually seen Glory Newcombe running away. He had taken quite a beating to the head over the past few days and might have been mistaken. The woman he had seen running away had definitely hit him, but had it been Glory? Or had he imagined seeing her? Had it been someone who only looked like her?

Slocum grew disgusted with himself for asking these questions. It had been Glory Newcombe in the whorehouse, and she had not been imprisoned as the Chinese women had. That left only one conclusion, and it didn't set well at all. The ride to the Presidio seemed over in a flash, because he dreaded what he had to do once he got there.

Slocum drew rein at the gate and looked down at the eager young soldier standing guard. He nodded in the private's direction, waiting for permission to enter the army post.

"Howdy, Mr. Slocum," greeted Private Carpenter. "You lookin' fer the captain?"

"I am," he answered. "You always on guard duty?"

The private looked sheepish, then said, "I get into so much trouble, I draw a whale of a lot o' extra duty. Wish I could be more like my buddy in the mess hall."

"What was his name? Kendricks?"

"He's got a soft job, cookin'—if that's what you call what he does to meat and potatoes. Might be I should try to be a cook, too. Leastways, I'd be sure to get all the food I wanted. But dealin' with so much garbage, well, reckon I'll keep standin' guard duty."

Slocum hardly heard the young soldier going on about his life in the army. He looked straight ahead along the road leading to the headquarters building, wondering if he would find Glory there pleading her case to her father. Or if she had simply hightailed it, knowing there could never be a good explanation for why she had been in a Chinese whorehouse.

"You see Miss Newcombe come in?" Slocum asked, cutting off the boy's long-winded reflections on life in the army.

"What's that? Oh, no, Mr. Slocum. I ain't see hide nor hair of her all day. And believe you me, if that purty lady'd come in, I'd of noticed right away." Carpenter blushed and looked uncomfortable. "You won't tell the adjutant or the colonel what I jist said, will you? It's not right fer a lowly private to say things like that 'bout such a purty woman."

"And one whose brother and father are your superiors," Slocum finished for the young man. "Don't worry none about it. My lips are sealed."

"You're a prince among men, Mr. Slocum. Wish everyone was like you."

Slocum rode on, leaving Private Carpenter to stand

watch. He reined back in front of the HQ building, not wanting to go in and having to. He was getting a better picture of what was happening at the Presidio, and it wasn't very pretty. Slocum dismounted and went inside, turning toward the colonel's office. A quick glance into the spacious suite of rooms showed that the post commander was out. Even his orderly had abandoned his desk for the moment. That left Caleb's office at the other end of the hall. Slocum walked down the corridor as if marching to his own execution. He even counted the paces, and stopped at thirteen in front of the adjutant's doorway.

He had hoped Caleb might also be out on duty, but the man sat behind his desk, not moving a muscle.

"Caleb, I need to talk with you a spell." Slocum stepped into the office and closed the door behind him. His eyebrows rose when he saw the sorry condition his friend was in. When he had gone into the city earlier, Caleb had been sweating and pale but functioning as an officer. Now he was downright corpselike.

"Can't it wait, John?"

"Nope, need to talk now." Slocum sank into the hard wooden chair facing Caleb's desk. The room turned suddenly stuffier for that simple action. He felt as if he were trapped with a wild, if injured, beast, and that was never a description he had considered for Caleb Newcombe before. Caleb might have been a hesitant officer in the field, but he was never bewildered and distracted as he was now. For Slocum, that boiled down to one simple fact: Caleb knew of his sister's involvement in the slave trading.

"Get you a drink?" Caleb reached into a bottom desk drawer and pulled out an almost empty bottle. His hands shaking, he poured a drink into a tin cup and quickly knocked it back, not waiting to find out if Slocum wanted a shot, too.

"You've been hitting the bottle mighty hard, haven't you? Is there a reason for that?"

"Nothing wrong with a bracer now and then," Caleb said. This certainly explained the officer's pitiful condition.

"You know about Glory, don't you?"

"What about her? She down there pourin' her sweet, poisonous lies into our father's ear again? All the time settin' him against me. *She* ought to be post adjutant."

"She's mixed up with the gang bringing Chinese slaves across the Presidio and then selling them in town." Slocum watched the shock spread on Caleb's face like some evil fungus. It was as if this was something the captain had never even considered.

"You lyin' sack of shit," Caleb cried. "How dare you say such a terrible thing about my sister? Glory might not look after my best interests, but she's no slave trader; it's not in her. I thought you were my friend!" Caleb tried to stand, but his legs gave way under him. He collapsed back into his chair and glared at Slocum as if he were the source of all the trouble at the Presidio.

"She was at a whorehouse near Chinatown," Slocum said carefully, "when I rescued the women being held inside."

"You're lying," Caleb said. He swallowed hard and looked as if he might puke at any instant. But he changed his tune a little when he said, almost plaintively, "There's some reason. Her damn charity work. That's what it is. She was there bein' charitable to the downtrodden."

"She was there because she was profiting off their being held against their will and sold as nickel-and-dime whores." Slocum ducked when Caleb lost his temper and threw the tin cup at his head, spilling what little liquor remained in the cup all over the desk. Jumping to his feet, Slocum leaned over the adjutant's desk and grabbed him by the front of his already rumpled uniform.

"You asked me to poke my nose into this. I didn't know what I'd find, but I never thought your sister would be in it up to her ears. I'm telling you straight, Caleb: Glory is mixed up in the slave selling, and maybe even running that whorehouse. I don't much care if you believe me, but it's the truth."

"Get out of here. Get the hell out of my office!"

"Whatever happened to the officer I knew out in New Mexico?"

"He's dead. Get out. Get out!" Caleb broke down and sobbed.

Slocum shoved Caleb backward into his chair and stared at the man, wondering what was wrong with him. The pasty white complexion had been dotted with sweat before; now Caleb's skin was as parched as the Mojave Desert, and his eyes burned with an unnatural light. Slocum left without another word, but he didn't go far. He gathered up the reins on his horse and led the animal to the side of the headquarters building and waited. It was getting near sunset, and Slocum wanted to see what Caleb did. He didn't have long to wait.

The Presidio adjutant left the building, stumbling as he walked, close to being falling-down drunk. He steadied a mite as he went to the stables and saddled his horse, but Slocum saw how Caleb weaved about and almost fell off once he mounted.

Slocum rode slowly after Caleb as the officer left the Presidio and headed down toward the Barbary Coast. It was dark enough for the lamplighters to come out and tease the gaslights into a warm yellow glow. This kept Caleb in easy view, and Slocum saw that the captain never bothered looking back to see if anyone trailed him. Slocum was not surprised when Caleb rode through the edges of the Barbary Coast section of town and headed for the center of Chinatown.

Slocum expected Caleb to make a beeline for the whorehouse, but the adjutant surprised him by going down a dark alley off Dupont Gai. Pausing in the mouth of the alley, Slocum saw Caleb dismount and walk on unsteady feet to a door, where he knocked. From his vantage in the street, Slocum couldn't hear what was said, but the door opened a crack and Caleb slipped inside.

Slocum scratched his head, wondering what was going on. If Caleb had wanted to go on a bender, any gin mill in the Barbary Coast would have sufficed. That he had come here so directly, never looking around, never showing any hesitation as to his destination, meant only one thing: Caleb Newcombe had succumbed to the lure of chasing the dragon. He was an opium addict. Slocum had started down the alleyway to root Caleb from the opium den when the door opened again. Out of the smoky interior stumbled two men, one supporting the other.

Slocum backtracked fast and watched the best he could as shadows cloaked the men. He recognized them both was they rode out, one in front of the other and both barely able to stay mounted.

Caleb Newcombe had gone into the opium den to get his father. It wasn't Caleb who was the opium addict, but Colonel Lawrence Newcombe.

17

"They will die," Mei Ling said firmly. The woman sat on an ornately carved teakwood chair, arms resting comfortably on either side of her trim body, legs crossed chastely at the ankles as she leaned back almost indolently. She wore a loose, shimmering green silk blouse and the baggy trousers favored by the Chinese women Slocum had seen around Chinatown. She might have been the Empress herself dealing out a verdict of death.

"That's easy to say, but you should want to catch them all alive," Slocum said.

"Why is this? These people enslave mine and do not deserve to live."

Slocum considered his words carefully. He felt as if *he* were on trial, but he knew he was instead defending the men—and the woman, Glory Newcombe—responsible for these heinous crimes.

"Killing the soldiers guarding the slaves as they're moved from the coast across the Presidio and into Chinatown isn't the way to stop them."

"If they are dead, they will enslave no more," Mei Ling said, a flash of anger coming now that he dared to disagree. Slocum saw she was not a woman who was lightly

156

crossed, probably even on the most trivial of matters. Back in China she might have been little more than a highly prized prostitute, but she obviously wielded considerable power in that position. She had brought that power with her to San Francisco.

"If they're killed," Slocum explained, "the ones responsible will only recruit more underlings. You need to chop off the head of this monster to stop it. To do that you must be certain you know who is responsible. The men guarding the slaves can be made to tell you who they work for." Slocum saw the anger die in Mei Ling's dark eyes and wondered if she thought, even for a second, that he defended the slavers because they were white.

"That is a wise thought," Mei Ling said, folding her hands in her lap and once more looking as relaxed as a cat basking in warm sunlight. "What are we to do?"

"We need to consider this from several directions," Slocum said. "The colonel isn't able to keep discipline among his troops, not with his opium addiction. The drug makes him crazy and prone to wild-ass behavior. Had you known Colonel Newcombe was smoking opium?"

Mei Ling inclined her head slightly, giving Slocum about all the answer he was likely to get. The woman gathered threads of information and spun them into a tapestry, much as Madame Lysette did. The difference came in their sources. Mei Ling tapped into events in Chinatown and along the docks, whereas Madame Lysette moved in upper-crust San Francisco society, only occasionally dropping down into the lower elements of the Barbary Coast. Their information might overlap, but not enough for the two of them to ever forge an alliance. Slocum thought that was just as well, considering the animus each held for the other. Individually, they were useful; together it was like juggling bottles of nitroglycerin.

"I don't think his son is high enough in rank to really be effective. While a post adjutant carries some command responsibility, he is more of an administrative officer. I don't know who the officers are above Captain Newcombe." Slocum didn't explain that this was less than truthful and that Caleb had lost whatever authority he might have had because of hitting the bottle so hard. Whether he drank himself into oblivion due to his father's addiction, his sister's behavior or his own inability to cope with the pressure of command, Slocum neither knew nor cared. Caleb Newcombe was a drunk, and useless when it came to stopping the slavers.

"I have dealings with a few of the Presidio officers. They are poltroons and wastrels, the lot. None can be depended upon for the action required," Mei Ling solemnly assured him. Slocum had been afraid of this. Caleb wouldn't have come to him in the first place if any of the senior officers were capable of investigating and stopping the phantom infestation that plagued the Presidio.

"Any opium addicts?"

"One major chases the dragon. Both lieutenant colonels are drunkards and spend most of their time at gambling halls and melodeons attempting to obtain free sex. They are seldom successful." Mei Ling spoke in an even tone, but Slocum saw her distaste for the Westerners in her face. He didn't much blame her. There were hundreds of military officers of all ilk left in the service after the war, but most were political animals more inclined to social climbing or outright debauchery than skilled service. The strategists and field tacticians were gone, replaced by garrison soldiers. And service in San Francisco presented more opportunity for dissolution than at other frontier forts.

At least that's the way it seemed at the Presidio. From what Slocum had seen, Fort Point isolated itself and kept its enlisted men and officers more alert and honest. How this had come about rested surely at Lawrence Newcombe's feet, since he was in charge of both posts.

"Caleb worried about the inspector general coming. The

IG ought to be of high enough rank to order out soldiers to stop the slavers and to find the ringleader," said Slocum.

"The inspector general arrives this evening," Mei Ling said. "One must assume that he is not involved in the slave trade, but how do you propose to reach him with your concerns?"

"Can't," Slocum admitted. "An IG isn't going to hold court and talk to civilians. He's here on specific business, and the problem of Chinese slavery isn't on that list— unless he can be convinced Presidio officers are involved."

"If he chooses to discharge such an investigation, your Colonel Newcombe's career is at an end. Perhaps also that of your friend, Captain Newcombe."

"Then that's the way it'll have to be," Slocum said decisively. He wanted an end to this and he wanted it soon. Caleb had to look after himself, even if he had been the one who had set Slocum onto the putrid scent of the slave traders. "Can your sources find when and where the inspector general is going to be here so I can try to get word to him?"

"You will destroy the careers and reputations of your friends to stop this slavery?" Mei Ling fixed him with her dark eyes. Her tone dared him to deny he would do such a thing.

"Yes."

"You are different from most Western men, John Slocum," she said as she rose gracefully from the elaborately wrought chair. She crossed the room, slowly undressing as she came to him.

"Not that I'm unwilling," Slocum said, watching as more and more of her sleek, satiny skin revealed itself to his lustful gaze. "But is this the time for it? We've got to get—" His protests were smothered by Mei Ling's lips, after she'd shed the blouse and stood naked to the waist before him.

She kissed him hard, then bit his lower lip, drawing it back slightly before releasing it.

"We can do nothing until complete darkness has settled. My messengers need to learn the inspector general's schedule. There is much to do, but nothing is left for us except to pass the time." Mei Ling kissed him again, tentatively, as if begging his approval for what she proposed.

"This looks like a mighty fine way of passing time," Slocum said. Mei Ling kissed him again, but this time Slocum didn't refuse what was being so wantonly offered. He reached out and ran his fingers over her flanks, tracing ribs and then working lower until he slipped his hands under the baggy trousers. With a smooth movement, he pulled the trousers over Mei Ling's buttocks and hips and let the flimsy garment slither slowly down her legs. She wore nothing under the trousers.

Slocum bent forward and kissed at small, amber globes capped with blood-engorged nipples. He toyed with them until another portion of the anatomy drew him like a magnet. Slocum kissed his way down her muscled, flat belly, dipping briefly into the well of her navel on his way, then worked lower with great deliberation. Seated as he was in the chair, bending this far proved difficult.

Mei Ling helped by stepping up onto the rungs of his chair, lifting her hips so she presented herself at face level.

Slocum reached around and cupped the half-moons of her rump and pulled her into his face. Crinkly fur scented with jasmine greeted him. He thrust out his tongue and lapped like a cat going after a saucer of cream, then raked the length of her slightly parted nether lips and plunged inward past them, swirling about in her tightness, Slocum tasted the saltiness of her core and wanted more. He kept at his tasty mission until Mei Ling let out tiny trapped-animal noises. She braced herself against his shoulders and arched her back, shoving her hips forward even more.

Slocum thrust his oral organ out as far as he could and gave her a good tongue-lashing. At the same time he began massaging the meaty lumps in his grip, pulling them apart and then crushing them to provoke a motion of flesh around his tongue unlike anything he had ever before experienced. The woman's strong inner muscles began to respond. Slocum kept lapping and licking and rubbing his nose up and down her pubes until Mei Ling let out a sharp gasp, followed by a low cry of stark pleasure.

Even then Slocum continued, but the woman began to sink down lower, as ecstasy robbed her of strength. Reluctantly, Slocum let her sag, but she was not done. As she sank lower, she reached down and hurriedly stripped away his gun belt and deftly opened his jeans to let his massive pole of man flesh leap upward.

"Let me get out of them," Slocum said, starting to lift her away so he could stand and shuck off the unwanted clothing.

"No, no," Mei Ling said in a husky voice. "I need you. Now. No time—I want you!"

She shoved him back down into the chair, his pants hobbling his ankles. With an agile twist, she knelt so her knees were on either side of his thighs as he sat in the chair. She lowered herself slowly until he felt the tip of his organ touch where his tongue had been seconds earlier.

Slocum grunted in satisfaction when Mei Ling settled down, her crotch pressing into his. He was entirely inside her hot, damp interior, and for a minute or more that was plenty good enough for both of them. Then they both wanted—needed—more.

Mei Ling began rotating her hips in small, deliberate circles that tugged and pulled at the roots of Slocum's manhood. He lifted off the chair by arching his back, trying to drive himself even farther into her most intimate recess, but the woman backed away, deliberately robbing him of this pleasure.

"Sit, enjoy. I will do for you what you have so ably done for me."

Mei Ling's hips began moving again, small subtle motions as she corkscrewed her way downward to once more take him fully within her. She leaned forward so he could kiss and suckle at her small, tempting breasts, but the real action occurred lower, at their groins. Slocum gasped when she began tensing and relaxing those wonderfully trained inner muscles, massaging his entire length until he felt as if he would explode at any instant. Just as he reached the point of no return, Mei Ling slowed and backed away, allowing him to savor the sensation before recovering his control. Again and again she did this, building his tensions until he thought he could not stand it any longer, then letting him recuperate.

She masterfully guided him closer to the brink of ecstasy, but never pushed him over it.

Slocum began a campaign to give as much as he was getting. Fingers probing, tongue licking, lips kissing and teeth gently nipping, he worked over every square inch of naked skin he could reach. By her short, sharp intakes of breath, he knew he was arousing her in the same fashion she was getting to him.

Together they continued their explorations and foreplay, until Mei Ling's body shivered as if she had contracted a fever.

"I . . . I cannot go on. You must . . . You must . . ."

Slocum knew what they both needed. And he delivered it. Raising his butt off the chair, he rammed upward, straight into her. He felt the carnal friction of his movement build. He thrust faster. She shivered and shook in reaction around him, clinging fiercely as he began pistoning like a fleshy machine. The heat of movement spread throughout his loins and then caused the explosion deep inside that could not be denied. As he spilled his load, he felt the woman tense. Locked together at the waist, they were both swept up in a powerful physical and emotional storm of their own making.

Delightfully exhausted from their mutual striving, they

silently shared the chair for several minutes, lost in their own private world of satiation. Mei Ling had turned about and sat on Slocum's lap, but eventually she stood and began picking up her discarded clothing. She bent over, facing away from him, giving him an exciting view.

He reached out and grabbed her around the waist and pulled her back to sit on his lap. This time they faced in the same direction.

"You said we had time. How *much* time?"

Mei Ling started to protest, then laughed like the ringing of small, syncopated silver bells when he did not release his grip around her slim waist.

"We have enough time. Do you have enough . . . ?" She reached down between her legs and sought that portion of Slocum's anatomy that had performed so well. "You do! Truly, not even the Emperor was so—"

"I don't want to hear about the damned Emperor," Slocum said. His hands moved upward and cupped the woman's apple-sized breasts and began squeezing down on the still-rigid nips capping them. "I don't want to hear anything but you calling out my name."

"Westerners," Mei Ling said with some disgust, but Slocum continued to stroke and fondle and regained rigidity, and her tone had changed when she gasped out, "*Westerners!*"

By the time they finished again, Mei Ling's messengers had returned with the information Slocum needed.

18

"He's inside but he refuses to see me," Slocum said, shaking his head. It was just as he had thought. The inspector general had arrived on the evening tide from inspections down south along the coast and had gone directly to Fort Point to begin his local tour. Slocum had presented himself to the guards at the heavy wooden gate blocking off the interior of the fort and had asked for the officer, only to be pointedly chased off. Even invoking Caleb Newcombe's name produced no results.

"The general can't be bothered" was the reply he got. He had insisted and the guards had become more physical in their effort to get rid of an annoyance.

He ruefully touched the spot on his belly where one guard had used his bayonet to poke and prod him along his way. Slocum had left because two other sentries had had their rifles leveled, with him in their sights. However he got a message to the IG, it wasn't going to be through the front gate and past the efficient guards.

"When does he go to the Presidio?" asked Mei Ling, amused at Slocum's pointed failure. She reached out and touched the spot where the bayonet had been jabbed, then lightly brushed her fingertips over a spot lower down, as if

164

telling him he was lucky the guard had not been careless with his bayonet. "Your friend can get you onto that post so you can speak with the many-starred general."

"Caleb was so far in his cups, I doubt if he can stand up anymore, much less issue a coherent order," Slocum said. Caleb Newcombe had too much on his plate to deal with. His father was an opium addict and desertion at the Presidio was at a critical level because so many soldiers had become frightened by the phantom parade. Either of those facts would alert the inspector general that the post was sorely in need of a complete change of command, if not outright courts-martial for the current officers.

"You do not approve of your friend's behavior," Mei Ling said. She thrust her hands out of sight into the sleeves of the robe she had donned over her more conventional outfit.

"A man has to deal with his problems however he can. If he wants to get drunk later, that's his business." Slocum found himself disgusted with Caleb over his excessive drinking. Swilling whiskey was no way for anyone to solve the troubles facing him.

"You are a strange man, John Slocum," Mei Ling said. "Drunkenness is not allowed in my service as it is in your people's."

"But it's all right to get all stupid smoking opium?" he shot back. He was sorry he had lost his temper with Mei Ling, but she had touched a sore spot. Slocum wanted to do more for Caleb, but there wasn't anything he could do to save the man or his career now.

"This might surprise you, but most customers to the opium dens are not Chinese. Some are, many are not. Colonel Newcombe is not unique."

Slocum stared up at the towering walls around Fort Point and knew he could never scale those four-story stone ramparts without falling or being spotted by a guard and shot down.

"Fog comes," Mei Ling said. She made a sweeping gesture, as if summoning it. Slocum saw a small army of highbinders appear out of the shadows, all approaching the fort.

"Get them out of sight," he said hastily. "If the guards see them, they'll open fire, It'll show the inspector general how alert they are." Slocum never saw the woman's second hand command, but the hatchet men all faded back into the darkness.

"Will there be more of your phantoms this night?" The way Mei Ling spoke made the question moot. She would hunt for them whether he agreed to join her or went his own way. Slocum cast one last glance up to the top of the high stone walls surrounding Fort Point and knew he was at a dead end here. Besides, she was right. The fog was already swirling about the bay, forming gray curtains that confused sight and robbed sound of its carrying power, then drifting ashore to stalk anything on land. If more slaves were to be brought into San Francisco, tonight would be perfect.

"It'd take quite a lot of brass to try slipping shackled prisoners across the Presidio with the IG here." A crooked smile curled his lips. Such impudence and even outright arrogant disregard was exactly what he expected. "Let's go. The one sure route they always take is up the far side of the Presidio and across the cemetery into town."

"The shoreline is long and difficult to search thoroughly," Mei Ling said. "We will wait in the cemetery for the kidnapped victims to be herded through."

They trooped along the streets and reached the foot of the hill leading up to the Presidio. Slocum knew that the road through the post would be guarded well. The rest of the perimeter might be less secure, if the sentries feared encountering the phantoms again. He pointed out dirt paths leading to the sprawling expanse of the cemetery and had the eerie feeling of sending ghosts of his own into the night. The highbinders glided past him, vanishing into the gathering fog to find hiding places.

"Where should we wait?" asked Mei Ling.

"You should wait in your quarters back in Chinatown. It might get rough out here. I want to see this ended tonight. If I can capture one or two of the soldiers, I can find out who is behind the slave smuggling."

"Your voice is strange. You know who is responsible, who profits from selling the flesh of stolen-away Celestials." Mei Ling peered at him from the dark. He couldn't see her ebony eyes but knew she fixed him with their steely stare.

"I have my suspicions, but there's nothing I could prove in court."

"We will not allow those responsible to reach a court, where their influence might result in acquittal. This is San Francisco. The courts are less than honest."

"We can go across to the Pacific coast and try to intercept the traffic there," Slocum said, ignoring what Mei Ling had said. For his own reasons, he didn't want the people responsible to go to trial, either. Better to see this through without drawn-out legal proceedings that would accomplish nothing but creating more ill will. The Chinese in town would never trust any jail sentence meted out, and Slocum knew it would never be enough punishment for the sorrow and suffering the slavers had caused.

"We stay," the woman said firmly. He knew that they were only guessing about the slave runners' motives tonight. There might not be a sailing ship arriving from the Orient with slaves to unload; the fear of the IG might be too great. There might not be a ready market for slaves, men or women, in Chinatown. Slocum's head began to ache with all the possibilities, not many of them ending well tonight. Worst might be not finding the slavers and their prisoners because they had moved their operation elsewhere.

Slocum's gut told him there would be another shipment tonight to replace those women who had been held in sex-

ual slavery and then freed. And they would follow the path
known best to them, from the Pacific coast through the Presidio cemetery. From what he could tell, as many as three
ships a day were arriving from the Flowery Kingdom, and
any of them might have a hold filled with unwilling sojourners. More than this, the fog was a perfect cover this
time of year, Slocum reflected as thick gray tendrils looped
around the equally cold marble tombstones and hid the
path leading uphill to the Presidio.

If the phantoms were to appear, it would be tonight.

"This looks to be a good place to wait," Slocum said,
sitting on a granite marker over a grave. He slipped the
leather keeper off the hammer of his six-gun and made
sure the pistol slid easily in the holster.

"The fog is thicker here than in Chinatown," Mei Ling
observed. "Sounds are muffled."

"Not that one," Slocum said, dropping to the ground
and putting his ear to the dirt. Through the packed earth he
heard the steady movement of feet. "They're coming. Get
your men ready."

Mei Ling made the gestures in the air that she had before. Slocum reckoned the highbinders were well trained to
watch for this signal and knew how to respond. If not, they
might lose the slavers again.

"There." Mei Ling reached into the folds of her voluminous sleeves and drew out a small pistol. She turned uphill and faced the wedge of fog drifting down from higher
elevation as it slipped up from the Pacific and over the
Presidio.

From the point of that foggy wedge came a ghostly figure of a soldier, white-faced with sunken, dark eyes and
hands that almost glowed as they clutched a rifle.

"Not yet," Slocum said urgently. "We need to see how
many we're facing."

It was too late, whether because Mei Ling had already
given the signal or because one of her hatchet men simply

got buck fever, it didn't matter. Hatchets cartwheeled through the air. One bounced off the leading phantom's rifle, causing it to discharge. A second hatchet sank deeply into the ghost's upper arm, producing a cry of completely human pain, followed by a stream of curses. The horde of highbinders rushed forward, confident of their easy victory against such mortal foes.

"Get 'em back!" Slocum's warning fell on deaf ears as the Celestials rushed ahead. They had scented blood and rushed in for the kill. From experience with the phantoms, Slocum knew how wrong they were.

The tong warriors ran smack into withering rifle fire from deeper in the fog bank.

Slocum reached out and grabbed Mei Ling's arm, keeping her from firing. She looked at him, venom in her eyes.

"You save them!"

"I don't want their prisoners hurt. If you can't see who you're shooting at, you're likely to kill the people you're trying to save."

The rifle fire continued to take its toll on the highbinders. Mei Ling shouted in Chinese and got her men to retreat.

"What should we do?"

"Let me scout ahead and see what we're up against." Slocum cursed as he went because the Chinese had jumped the gun and ruined his planned ambush. If the line of prisoners had reached the more open section of the cemetery from the forested area where they were now held, picking off the "phantoms" would have been easier. Now the slavers could use their victims as shields and shoot at anyone trying to cross the cemetery.

Slocum darted this way and that, keeping low and using the same fog to hide his advance that had curtained the slavers. He reached the scraggly trees at the edge of the forest and peered into the foggy dark. At first he saw nothing. Then movement. Small but distinct. And in that direction he saw a floating white oval. Slocum moved as quietly as any Indian toward the phantom, then launched himself through the air as the man turned, rifle coming to bear.

Slocum crashed into the phantom and found it suitably substantial. He bore the man backward until they smashed into a tree trunk. The ersatz phantom was momentarily stunned by the impact, giving Slocum the chance he needed. He brought his knee up hard into the man's groin. As the slaver bent double Slocum lifted his knee again into the exposed chin. A dull *crack* told that the man wasn't going to be a problem any longer.

Kneeling, Slocum rolled the man over. The dead man wore a standard-issue blue wool uniform, but his face was well dusted with flour. Soot around the eyes produced a sunken, dead look in the middle of the stark white flour makeup. Adding to the eeriness, the fog condensed on the flesh and caused tiny pockmarks to appear in the flour on the man's cheeks and forehead. Slocum looked at the man's hands and couldn't figure out what they had been dipped in to provide the faint luminescent lightning bug look. Some of it had transferred to the rifle, which Slocum scooped up and checked. Only a couple rounds remained in the magazine.

He left his investigation of the no-longer-unknown phantom and slipped deeper into the woods. When he heard soft moaning sounds he knew he was close to the prisoners, and headed in that direction.

As suddenly as any real ghost might appear, another of the phantoms materialized out of the fog. Slocum got off the first shot but missed. The soldier fired and drove Slocum back down the hill in the direction of the cemetery. This was dangerous ground for him, since the highbinders might mistake him for one of the slavers, but Slocum had no other choice. The man was shouting for his comrades to come to his aid. If he stayed any longer, Slocum knew, he would be facing four or five marksmen.

He slipped on the damp grass and went facedown onto

the ground, rolled to his back and fired without a target. He didn't dare let them come up close enough behind to get a good shot at him or he'd be a goner. His round went screaming into the fog but had the worst result possible: Instead of keeping the phantoms at bay, it drew them. He had somehow blundered along and lost them—until his shot had let them find him.

Slocum saw four ghostly, ghastly figures coming toward him. He fired again, then the rifle he had taken came up empty. He fumbled for his six-shooter but knew there was no way he could get them all before one fired the bullet that would rob him of his life.

A new sound crashed through in the fog. Slocum had heard shooting and the clanking of chains and even the hushed singsong of Chinese being spoken, probably by the prisoners. Now it was all drowned out by the thunder of horses' hooves.

Slocum blinked in disbelief. Where the slavers had been circling to kill him, now they ran about wildly, screaming and shouting—and through the fog came a full-scale cavalry charge. Slocum tried to guess at how many troopers rode down on the slavers. Enough to protect a company of men.

He scrambled to his feet and ran downhill into the cemetery and immediately found Mei Ling.

"What is going on?" she asked. "There is such an uproar."

"Get your hatchet men out of here," Slocum said. "The cavalry's arrived."

"The boat landing the imprisoned ones," Mei Ling said. "It will escape. We must—"

Slocum grabbed her, planted a kiss on her lips to silence her, then pushed the stunned woman back.

"It'll all be taken care of. I promise. Now get the hell out of here. Those soldiers won't know the difference between you and your men and the prisoners."

"You will see that they are released?"

"Go!" This time Mei Ling obeyed. A wistful smile came to her lips, then she bowed slightly and vanished into the fog. Slocum heard her calling to the highbinders, getting them organized and moving back into Chinatown where they would be safe. Then he turned to see what progress the cavalry troopers were making against the slavers.

The fog parted like the Red Sea, giving Slocum a better look at the fight going on from one side of the cemetery to the other. The horse-mounted soldiers shot from their superior height at the men hunkered down on the ground and took refuge behind tombstones.

A loud battle cry sounded. Through the fog, riding like a fiend, galloped Colonel Lawrence Newcombe, sword held high. He rushed past the other soldiers in the mounted unit as he led a frontal assault on the remaining slavers.

Slocum called to the colonel, tried to warn him, drew his six-shooter and fired until the hammer fell on a spent chamber—to no avail. A phantom figure stood, took aim and fired accurately. The colonel flew from the saddle and tumbled backward to the ground. After he hit with a solid thud, he lay unmoving.

Slocum began reloading, intent on getting to the man who had shot the colonel from the saddle. But Slocum never finished his job, for on the heels of the colonel's attack came another rider. Caleb Newcombe screeched like an Apache warrior as he bent low and swung his heavy saber. The blade landed hard on the phantom rifleman's shoulder. Caleb rode past as the ersatz ghost dropped his carbine and clutched at his broken collarbone.

This was the last of the battle. The mounted soldiers were regrouped by a ramrod-straight officer who barked commands with both skill and intent. The cavalry troopers quickly rounded up the few men still standing and corralled them.

Slocum considered what he ought to do now that the

slavers were under arrest. The decision was made for him when Caleb trotted over. The man's face was as white and pinched as it had been when he was hitting the bottle, but now there was a pain born not of the physical, but of the emotional.

"Your pa's dead," Slocum said. He looked to where the colonel lay unmoving, half draped over a tombstone. There was no way he could have survived. If the bullet hadn't killed the army commander outright, the fall would have. Lawrence Newcombe's head was canted at an unnatural angle.

"I know." Caleb sat a little straighter in the saddle. "I warned him not to come tonight but he insisted, even in his weakened condition. At least he died like a soldier."

"In front of the inspector general," Slocum said, watching the stiff officer as he rode about. He caught the glint of distant light off the general's stars on his epaulets.

"He won't get a star of his own, but he isn't going to be disgraced, either." Caleb looked around. "It was Sergeant Thomassen who shot him. I recognized the sergeant when I attacked with my sword. He was in command of the slavers—the phantoms I'd been so worried about."

"I figured he was one of them," Slocum said.

"One? He was the ringleader. We saw how he commanded the others. Two of his gang were among the deserters. I suspect others listed as deserting might have been killed so they wouldn't turn on him, or maybe they'll wind up having been in the gang. One thing is certain: Thomassen will stand in front of a firing squad for this utter disgrace to our unit."

"Good," Slocum said. "What are you going to do now?"

"I need to be sure the prisoners are all secured in the stockade, probably at Fort Point, until I am sure we have all of the slavery ring rooted out in the Presidio. Then there'll be the courts-martial. That'll be the end of this sordid affair. And the end of my career."

"What about the ringleader?" Slocum asked.

Caleb started at him and then asked, "What are you saying? Sergeant Thomassen is the one responsible. Don't talk foolishness, John." Caleb sounded sincere, making Slocum wonder how long a man, even one prone to drinking away his problems, could delude himself. The answer was seated on a horse before him. Caleb Newcombe could continue to deny his sister had anything to do with the slave smuggling forever.

Slocum checked his six-shooter and left Caleb to his roundup. He had the real leader to bring to justice, if the captain wasn't capable of it himself. Slocum hoped he wasn't too late.

19

It seemed like a thousand miles across the Presidio parade grounds and down the far side of the hill leading to the Pacific Ocean, but Slocum kept moving through the thinning fog with a grim determination. It was a fickle fog, hanging thick in places and giving fifty-yard vistas in others, but Slocum headed for the sound of the crashing surf. That kept him going in the right direction until he came to the beach. He wasn't sure the ringleader would be here, but he thought she would.

Then he saw her.

Glory Newcombe tried to scramble into the longboat as it was slipping off the beach and back into the surf, but the sailor in the prow prevented her from entering.

"Let me in!" Glory fought savagely to push the sailor back so she could tumble into the longboat, but he was stronger and had footing she lacked. He grabbed her by the upper arms and heaved, throwing her through the air to land half on the beach and half in the water. "You son of a bitch!" she screamed. "I can't stay here. Not now!"

Slocum advanced slowly, wary of how dangerous she could be. She had fooled him once. She would never do it a second time.

"The inspector general's waiting up at the HQ for you," Slocum said loudly enough to get the brunette's attention.

"You meddling fool. You've ruined everything," Glory cried. She twisted about, got her feet under her and tried to run. Her water-soaked skirts weighed her down and kept her from making very good speed. Within ten yards she fell down, worn-out from exertion and fear. Slocum had followed Glory at a more leisurely pace, letting her exhaust herself. He did not want to have the hellion fighting him the entire way back to the military post.

"Your father's dead," Slocum said as he neared her. She rested on hands and knees, panting like a dog. Glory tossed her hair about to get the wet strands out of her face and glared at him over her shoulder. Then her eyes changed from furious to cunning.

"He deserved it. And you deserve a reward, John. Come on, come get your reward. I'm waiting for you."

"Is that how you kept Thomassen and the others in line?"

"He was a fool! He thought I loved him. I hated him. I hated the others. All of them! I hated them because they were weak and stupid. But you're smart, John, and you're strong. That's what I enjoyed most about making love with you—your strength."

"Get up. That's not going to work now." He stayed just beyond her reach and was glad for his caution. She threw herself at him clumsily, hissing and spitting like an angry cat. Glory clawed wildly but Slocum stepped back a pace so she flopped in front of him, her attack missing by a country mile.

"You ruined it all. I wanted it for my father. He was never going to get another promotion, and it was killing him."

"When he realized that he would never be promoted to general, did he start smoking opium?"

"Yes," she hissed. "He was weak, just like the others, but

he was still commander of the post. He was so easily manipulated. He'd do anything I asked. All I had to do was tell him where he could get his damned opium in Chinatown."

"Why didn't you work your scheme at Fort Point? The boats could have unloaded their human cargo in the city that way."

"They think they're so good. An elite unit. But the tongs kept the ships from unloading the slaves anywhere along the Embarcadero. I came up with the idea of marching them from the Pacific shore into town. Discipline at the Presidio was sloppy, because of my weakling brother. When I heard one of his men complaining about phantoms, I knew how I could get the Chink slaves to the whorehouses."

"Yours?"

"Of course they were my brothels," Glory said, sneering. "I'm rich, John. I'll share it. We can go off together and—"

He reached down and grabbed her. With a jerk, he got her onto her feet and shoved her in the direction of the Presidio.

"It doesn't have to be this way, John. There's no proof against me. It was all Thomassen's doing; I can testify to that. If you go along, we can share all I've made."

"All you've made off the suffering of men and women who were kidnapped and brought halfway around the world. Go on, Glory. Move." He shoved her again. She walked hesitantly because of the soaked skirts weighing her down and from her exhaustion at trying to escape. "I doubt we'll ever find which captains of which ships brought the slaves, but maybe you'll tell us and get it off your soul before they hang you."

"They'll never hang me. Caleb won't let them. He's a 'pusillanimous pup,' as our father called him, but he believes me. I tell you, there's no proof. Don't get involved, John. Let me go."

He listened to her alternately pleading and threatening as they climbed the steep sloping path back to the Presidio parade grounds. Slocum had to move closer to her, as odious as that was to him, when the fog began to thicken again. He didn't want her trying to make another break for freedom. She had almost gotten away in the longboat. Only the sailor's reluctance to have a woman aboard his ship had kept her from making a clean getaway.

They marched out onto the foggy grounds. Near the HQ building Slocum thought he saw the IG and several officers gathered around him, though he couldn't be sure. But what he thought he saw was different from Glory's perception of the fog-shrouded tableau.

"No, my God, no!" She tried to bolt. He grabbed for her and tore away part of her sleeve. "They're coming for me. Phantoms are after me!"

Slocum recovered his balance and stared. Indistinct figures moved through the fog, arms outstretched as if they groped for the woman. She screamed and ran. A shot sounded. Glory Newcombe stumbled, fell to her knees, then simply crumpled to the ground without making another sound.

Slocum rushed forward and caught the arm of one of the indistinct figures in the fog. He found himself struggling with a highbinder.

"Let him go," came Mei Ling's soft voice. "We rescue those who were brought ashore tonight. Nothing more."

"But Glory. You killed her!"

"No," Mei Ling said, her voice becoming more distant. "I did not. None of my warriors harmed her." Then she and the hatchet men were hidden by the thick fog.

Slocum spun around, but was alone. He oriented himself and went to Glory's side. She lay on the ground. The bullet had caught her in the breast, drilling straight through her heart.

He looked up as the capricious fog parted, and saw

Caleb Newcombe standing like a chiseled marble statue, his still-smoking service pistol clutched in his hand. He was whiter than a bleached muslin sheet and hardly seemed to breathe.

"You shot your sister," Slocum said, marveling. "Did you know?"

Caleb said nothing as he holstered his six-shooter, came to attention, saluted stiffly, then did an about-face and marched off toward headquarters without saying a word. Slocum knew the officer's career was truly at an end, no matter what the IG's report. And Slocum's duty to Caleb Newcombe was at an end. He had stopped the phantoms stalking the Presidio.

The roundhouse punch missed Slocum's head by a fraction of an inch. He ducked low and came in, fists flying. He pounded against Big Pete Ordway's rock-hard belly until his fists ached, but he kept at it. The gambler slowly weakened as Slocum kept up his attack, ducking clumsy punches and returning with a flurry of his own. He finally saw his chance when the mountainous gambler stepped back to catch his breath. Slocum clasped his hands together into a giant fist and swung as if he were bringing an axe handle around. The shock rippled all the way to his shoulder as his fists connected with Big Pete's chin. The gambler's head snapped back, he stumbled and then he sprawled on the ground, unconscious.

Panting, Slocum turned and lifted his bloody, bruised fists in the direction of the Walensky brothers.

"You next? You want to dispute what I owe you?"

"You got a way about you, Slocum. Not like that welshing son of a bitch you called a partner."

Slocum glared at the gambler and stepped forward. "You agree that I don't owe you a damned cent?"

"Not one red cent," Gabe Walensky said hastily, glancing at his partner on the ground and at his brother Herk.

Then he smiled broadly and said, "Fact is, we just made twice what your partner owed us."

"What? How's that?"

Gabe Walensky pointed to the men in a large circle around them, all come to see the fight.

"Most of them fellas, see, they don't believe Big Pete could ever lose a bare-knuckles fistfight, especially to a skinny fella like you." Walensky lowered his voice into a conspiratorial whisper. "So me and Herk, we took some bets from 'em. Got damn good odds, too."

"You bet against your own partner?"

"Paid off, didn't it?"

"Burn in hell," Slocum said, pushing past the gamblers.

"No hard feelin's, Slocum. It's all business. Anytime you want to get into a game with us, you're welcome!" called Herk Walensky.

Slocum mounted his horse and sat astride for a moment, his hands hurting like fire. He flexed them a few times to get feeling back into them before taking the reins and riding for the Ferry Building. He had been in San Francisco long enough and wanted nothing more than endless blue sky and towering mountains and soft winds whispering through deserted meadows. There were too many people here for his liking, and they all worked a different swindle on him to get what they wanted. Glory Newcombe had trafficked in human flesh and had used her wiles to make him look elsewhere for the culprit that had turned out to be her. Caleb had been too ineffectual to find on his own the answers he sought. Colonel Newcombe had been prisoner to a vile, addictive vice.

Slocum was well delivered from San Francisco.

As he rode to the docks to wait for the ferry that would take him across the bay to Oakland so he could reach the Sierras by the end of the week, he saw two small knots of people waiting. They all turned when he rode closer. Slocum made sure his six-shooter was ready for action as he approached, then saw he wouldn't need to shoot his way out of this reception party.

To one side stood Mei Ling and several of her tong fighters. On the other side of the dock Madame Lysette waited with four of her soiled doves. Slocum recognized Lily right away. The woman appeared healthier than before. He thought the madam must have kept her off opium long enough for her to begin to recover from her drug-induced pallor. He rode to the strawberry blonde's side of the dock first, touched the brim of his hat and called, "You waiting for someone?"

"Why, Mr. Slocum," Madame Lysette said in her half-joking fashion, "you can be such a tease at times. You know it's you we've come to bid a fond farewell to. Isn't there any way we can induce you to stay for a while longer?"

"I kin make it real pleasurable fer ya, honey," Lily said. Her eyes were still drug-bright, but she had fleshed out delightfully in all the right places.

"You hush up, Lily. If he wants to stay, he's *mine*. I owe him so much."

Slocum touched the pocket where the thick wad of greenbacks still rode. He had nigh on a thousand dollars of Madame Lysette's paper money, given him to free her from jail. That she had not needed the money in order to be released, and did not need it now, did nothing to change the fact the money was hers.

Slocum took his hand away from his pocket. He had earned it. And more.

He just wasn't going to claim any further reward from the madam or any of her eager Cyprians.

"Consider the debt paid, Madame Lysette," Slocum said. "The ferry's coming," he said, hearing its steam whistle as the boat neared the dock. "I don't want to miss it."

"If you do, you can stay at my house," she said, grinning. Both of them knew he wouldn't accept such an offer. He touched the brim of his hat again and turned his horse's face to the other side of the dock, then rode over and dismounted.

"I hadn't expected so many folks to see me off," Slocum said to Mei Ling.

"We owe you a deep debt of gratitude," the Chinese woman said, bowing low.

"Did you get the prisoners away?"

"There are no more prisoners," she said obliquely. "We are also pleased that there will be no trials for those guilty of slave trading and forced prostitution."

Slocum started to ask what had happened to Sergeant Thomassen and the others, but held his tongue. He wanted to get away from such goings-on, not become more involved in what might have been outright murder of men locked up in jail cells. Whatever the Six Companies had decreed—whatever Mei Ling had ordered—was hardly punishment enough for the sergeant. And Glory Newcombe would never scheme again, thanks to her brother's accurate aim.

"You're the one thing I will miss in San Francisco," he said in a voice so low only Mei Ling could hear.

"And you are the one person whom I will miss. Should you ever return, please call on me. I will be certain you are greeted . . . warmly."

Slocum almost took Mei Ling in his arms and kissed her, but that would have caused a row among the highbinders guarding her. She was reason to stay in San Francisco, but he had even more compelling reasons to leave.

"Good-bye," he said. To his surprise, she moved quickly, came to him and fleetingly brushed her lips across his. Then she was gone, only a lingering scent of jasmine remaining to erode his determination to leave San Francisco.

Slocum heard the shocked gasps from Madame Lysette and her entourage at such a public display with a Chinese woman, but he didn't care. He led his horse to the ferry and waited to board. There were distant horizons calling—ones without all the intrigue he had found at the Presidio and in San Francisco.

Watch for

SLOCUM AND LADY DEATH

319th novel in the exciting SLOCUM series

from Jove

Coming in September!

Explore the exciting Old West with one of the men who made it wild!

LONGARM AND THE DEAD MAN'S TALE #300   0-515-13633-6
LONGARM AND THE BANK ROBBER'S DAUGHTER #301
                                            0-515-13641-7
LONGARM AND THE GOLDEN GHOST #302   0-515-13659-X
LONGARM AND THE GRAND CANYON GANG #303
                                            0-515-13685-9
LONGARM AND THE GREAT MILK TRAIN ROBBERY #304
                                            0-515-13697-2
LONGARM AND THE TALKING SPIRIT #305   0-515-13716-2
LONGARM AND THE PIRATE'S GOLD #306   0-515-13734-0
LONGARM AND THE OUTLAW'S SHADOW #307   0-515-13751-0
LONGARM AND THE MONTANA MADMEN #308   0-515-13774-X
LONGARM IN THE TALL TIMBER #309   0-515-13795-2
LONGARM SETS THE STAGE #310   0-515-13813-4
LONGARM AND THE DEVIL'S BRIDE #311   0-515-13836-3
LONGARM AND THE TWO-BIT POSSE #312   0-515-13853-3
LONGARM AND THE BOYS IN THE BACK ROOM #313
                                            0-515-13859-2
LONGARM AND THE COMSTOCK LODE KILLERS #314
                                            0-515-13877-0
LONGARM AND THE LOST PATROL #315   0-515-13888-6
LONGARM AND THE UNWELCOME WOOLIES #316
                                            0-515-13900-9
LONGARM AND THE PAIUTE INDIAN WAR #317   0-515-13934-3
LONGARM AND THE LUNATIC #318   0-515-13944-0
LONGARM AND THE SIDEKICK FROM HELL #319   0-515-13956-4
LONGARM AND THE TEXAS TREASURE HUNT #320
                                            0-515-13966-1

**AVAILABLE WHEREVER BOOKS ARE SOLD OR AT
PENGUIN.COM**

(Ad # B112)

J. R. ROBERTS
THE GUNSMITH